HARRIET E. WILSON

Our Nig

Or,

Sketches from the Life of a Free Black

Edited by
P. GABRIELLE FOREMAN *and* REGINALD H. PITTS

Introduction by
P. GABRIELLE FOREMAN

PENGUIN BOOKS

PENGUIN BOOKS

Published by the Penguin Group
Penguin Group (USA) Inc., 375 Hudson Street, New York, New York 10014, U.S.A.
Penguin Group (Canada), 90 Eglinton Avenue East, Suite 700, Toronto, Ontario, Canada M4P 2Y3
(a division of Pearson Penguin Canada Inc.)
Penguin Books Ltd, 80 Strand, London WC2R 0RL, England
Penguin Ireland, 25 St Stephen's Green, Dublin 2, Ireland (a division of Penguin Books Ltd)
Penguin Group (Australia), 250 Camberwell Road, Camberwell, Victoria 3124, Australia
(a division of Pearson Australia Group Pty Ltd)
Penguin Books India Pvt Ltd, 11 Community Centre, Panchsheel Park, New Delhi – 110 017, India
Penguin Group (NZ), 67 Apollo Drive, Rosedale, North Shore 0632, New Zealand
(a division of Pearson New Zealand Ltd)
Penguin Books (South Africa) (Pty) Ltd, 24 Sturdee Avenue, Rosebank, Johannesburg 2196, South Africa

Penguin Books Ltd, Registered Offices:
80 Strand, London WC2R 0RL, England

First published in the United States of America by Geo. C. Rand & Avery 1859
Edition with an introduction and notes by P. Gabrielle Foreman and Reginald H. Pitts
published in Penguin Books 2005
This edition with an expanded introduction and appendix published 2009

10

LIBRARY OF CONGRESS CATALOGING IN PUBLICATION DATA
Wilson, Harriet E., 1825–1900.
Our nig, or, Sketches from the life of a free black / Harriet E. Wilson / edited by P. Gabrielle Foreman and Reginald H. Pitts ; introduction by P. Gabrielle Foreman.
p. cm.—(Penguin classics)
Includes bibliographical references.
ISBN 978-0-14-310576-3
1. African American women domestics—Fiction. 2. African American women—Fiction. 3. Free African Americans—Fiction. 4. New England—Fiction. 5. Racism—Fiction. I. Foreman, P. Gabrielle (Pier Gabrielle) II. Pitts, Reginald H. III. Title. IV. Title: Our nig. V. Title: Sketches from the life of a free Black.
PS3334.W39O9 2009
813'.3—dc22 2009019511

Printed in the United States of America
Set in Sabon

Contents

Chronology I

Harriet E. "Hattie" Wilson
1825–1900

1825 (March 15). Harriet E. "Hattie" Adams ("Alfrado" or "Frado") born in Milford, New Hampshire, probably on the farm and cooperage of Timothy Blanchard ("Pete Greene"), to Joshua Green ("Jim"), an African American "hooper of barrels," and Margaret Adams, or Smith ("Mag Smith"), a white washerwoman, according to *Our Nig.*[1]

c. 1829. According to *Our Nig,* "Jim," Wilson's father, Joshua Green, dies.

1830. Is possibly the "white female aged under five years" enumerated in the household of Primus Chandler Jr., an African American resident of nearby Bedford, New Hampshire.[2]

1830–31. Abandoned by mother Mag (Margaret Adams or Smith) and her paramour at the Hayward home ("the Bellmonts") in Milford; serves as an indentured servant.[3]

1830 March. "Margaret Ann Smith," twenty-seven, from Portsmouth, New Hampshire, dies in Boston, after a violent and intoxicated quarrel with her black lover. The local Amherst/Milford paper carries a full announcement.

1832–34. Attends school (most likely at District School Number 3) for three months a year for three years. The Hayward Farm was located in that district according to the 1854 map of Milford by C. E. Potter.

1843 (January 4–5). Massive abolitionist rally including Parker Pillsbury, Stephen S. Foster, Nathaniel P. Rogers, The Hutchinson Family Singers, and the fugitives George Latimer and George Johnson, occurs in Milford.

1843 (October 11). John Gallatin Robinson, Wilson's second husband, born in Sherbrooke County, Quebec, Canada, son of Albert Gallatin Robinson and Jane S. (Sunbury) Robinson.[4]

1843 or 1846. Leaves the Haywards and goes to work as a servant for other families.

1846 (spring–fall). According to *Our Nig,* attempts to work for "Mrs. Moore" and "Mrs. Hale" (Mrs. Sarah Dexter Kimball) and falls ill; she is first removed to the Hayward household; after she recovers, she attempts to work again until her health fails.

1847. Nehemiah Hayward and wife Rebecca S. (Hutchinson) move to Baltimore.

1847–49. Listed as a town pauper and boards with "two maids (old)" (Fanny and Edna Kidder).[5]

1849–50. Listed as a town pauper and boards with "Mrs. Hoggs" (Mary Louisa [Barnes] Boyles).

1850 (after August). Moves to Ware or Worcester, Massachusetts, through the ministrations of an "itinerant colored lecturer," perhaps Thomas H. Jones. In Ware, she may have boarded with Mrs. Mary (Wrigley) Walker ("Mrs. Walker"). If in Worcester, she may have boarded with barber Gilbert Walker and his mother, Ann.[6]

1851. Harriet Adams and Thomas Wilson meet in "W——," Massachusetts. They marry in Milford, New Hampshire, on October 6.

1851 (December 6). Poem "Fading Away," by "Hattie," appears in local newspaper, the *Farmer's Cabinet.*[7]

1852 (January?). Moved to Hillsborough County Poor Farm in Goffstown, New Hampshire.

1852 (circa June 15). Son, George Mason Wilson, born at Poor Farm.[8]

1852 (spring–fall). Thomas Wilson returns, takes wife, Harriet, and George from Poor Farm to either Milford, Manchester, or Nashua, New Hampshire, then returns to sea, again leaving them destitute; they're probably again helped by Caleb and Laura Wright Hutchinson, who is possibly "Margaretta Thorn."

1853 (May 30). Thomas Wilson perhaps dies onboard sloop *Cabassa* of Portland, Maine, Captain Charles Littlejohn commanding, in the harbor of Cardenas, Cuba.[9]

1854–55. "Harriet E. Wilson and Child" on the Milford Poor List until she is able to make a small living for herself while George is placed with foster parents as a pauper.[10]

1855 (June–August). George M. Wilson forced to spend six weeks at Hillsborough County Poor Farm while mother lies ill, possibly in Springfield, Massachusetts.[11]

1855–59. Joshua and Irene Fisher Hutchinson may have taken George Wilson in as a pauper while Hattie traveled in central and western Massachusetts and southern New Hampshire, working as a seamstress, house servant, and selling her hair products, contingent on her health. During this period she begins to write, and then she publishes *Our Nig*.

1857–59 (September–April). Wilson begins advertising her hair products in the local paper, the *Farmer's Cabinet*. During this period she lives for a time in Nashua, New Hampshire, at 9 Winter Street and 13 Cottage Street.

1859 (August 18). *Our Nig* copyrighted, with a copy deposited in the Office of the Clerk of the U.S. District Court of Massachusetts.

1859 (September 5). *Our Nig* published by George C. Rand and Avery.

1859 (October 13). Calvin Dascomb, Sr. ("C. D. S."), dies in Wilton, New Hampshire.

1860 (February 15). George Mason Wilson dies in Milford, aged seven years, eight months.[12]

1860. Possibly working in cotton mill in Manchester, New Hampshire, boarding with Mrs. Sophia W. Young.[13]

1860–61. Harriet E. Wilson forms a business relationship with Henry P. Wilson (no relation), a white druggist eight years her junior who manufactures and sells her products in Manchester. Advertisements begin in larger papers in April 1860. By December 1861, different versions of Mrs. H. E. Wilson ads are running in seven states and in scores of papers.

1862. By the end of the year advertisements have tapered off. Henry P. Wilson becomes ill and is much less active in his business.

1863. Wilson begins to become more deeply involved with the growing Spiritualist movement. "Mrs. Wilson" (note there is no first name) is listed under "Support of County Paupers" in Hillsborough County, New Hampshire.[14]

1863–66. Possibly boarding with Laura Hutchinson until Hutchinson's marriage and move from New Hampshire in 1866; more than likely also involved with Eleanor "Betsy" (Knowlton) Came, Ellen (Travis) Booth, and Sarah H. (Bennett) Mixer, who were active as "trance readers," "clairvoyant physicians," and Spiritualists in Milford and environs.[15]

1867. Hattie Wilson listed in the Boston Spiritualist newspaper *Banner of Light* as living in East Cambridge, Massachusetts, and described as "the eloquent and earnest colored trance medium"; she later moves across the Charles River to 70 Tremont Street in Boston. She joins the Massachusetts Spiritualists Association where she participates in their semiannual conventions, sharing the podium with the famous Andrew Jackson Davis, and gives an address in favor of labor reform and the education of children in Spiritualist doctrine.

1867 (August 29–September 1). Is known in Spiritualist circles as "the colored medium." Attends a "Great Spiritualist Camp Meeting" in Pierpont Grove, Melrose, Massachusetts, where she delivers an address in front of as many as three thousand.

1868. Gives lectures, sometimes entranced, in Massachusetts, New Hampshire, Maine, and Connecticut. The *Banner of Light* reports that she "has been constantly and successfully engaged the past year in this vicinity as a healing medium and a trance speaker, and has won a host of friends. We cordially commend her to the hospitality of the spiritual brotherhood everywhere." Boston City Directory describes her as "Dr. Hattie E. Wilson." Moves to 150 Tremont Street, and later to 26 Carver Street, Boston.[16]

1869. Moves to 46 Carver Street, Boston, and works with John Gallatin Robinson, an apothecary. The 1870 Federal Census lists her as a thirty-eight-year-old white native of New Hampshire, who is a physician. Robinson, listed as a twenty-six-year-old native of Connecticut, who is also a physician, also lives at 46 Carver Street.[17]

1870 (September 29). John Gallatin Robinson and Harriet E. Wilson marry in Boston.[18] The record shows that "Harriet E. Wilson," born in Milford, New Hampshire, but resident in Boston, declared that she was thirty-seven [*sic*] years old (to her husband's twenty-six), white, and the daughter of Joshua and Margaret Green; this was her second marriage, her husband's first. The officiating minister was a Rev. J. L. Mansfield, a Spiritualist minister.

1870 (October 22–23). *Banner of Light* reports that at the quarterly convention of Spiritualists in Haverhill, Massachusetts, Wilson testifies to how she had been "brought into acquaintance with her father in spirit-life, who was her almost constant companion." She further said that "you will know that the spirit-world is not afar off, in space, but here in our midst; and that spirits are not bodiless beings but are with us in our homes."

1872–77. As "Mrs. Hattie E. Robinson," listed in the Boston Spiritualist newspaper *Banner of Light* as trance reader and lecturer at 46 Carver Street, off the Boston Common. She alternately continues to be referred to as "Mrs. Hattie E. Wilson." Continues being involved in musical entertainments at Spiritualist gatherings.

1873 (May). Works to establish a new Spiritualist society in Mansfield and Foxboro, Massachusetts.

1873 (August 13–17). Speaks with Victoria Woodhull and others at the Fourth Annual Spiritualist Camp Meeting, Silver Lake, Plympton, Massachusetts, where an estimated sixteen thousand people assemble. Is chosen as one of six Massachusetts delegates to attend the American Association of Spiritualists Convention in Chicago. Listed this year as both Mrs. Hattie E. Robinson and Hattie E. Wilson.

1873–74. Is active in the formation and maintenance of Children's Progressive Lyceums, which serve as Sunday schools for the children of Spiritualists. Is particularly active in Temple Hall and Rochester Hall. Speaks to children at a major gathering at New Fraternity Hall, March 31. Gives a speech at the wedding of the conductor, or leader, of the Children's Lyceum, No. 1, of Boston.[19]

1873–74. Hosts Spiritualist social events that are reported in the *Banner of Light*. Speaks at Silver Lake Camp Meeting, "under direct spirit control," giving an entertaining speech confirming the fitness of the previous speakers.[20]

1874 (September 15–18). Speaks against the "doctrine of turning of children over to the State" based on her own experiences as one "who never had a mother," and discusses her grievances with the conduct of some Boston Spiritualists at convention of Universal Association of Spiritualists in Boston. According to the *Banner of Light* the convention was "a mass meeting of Radicals and Reformers." The *Religio-Philosophical Journal* characterized it as a "mongrel convention" being held "under the call of the National Spiritualists Association of which Victoria Woodhull is the president."[21]

1876 (March 25). *Banner of Light* reports a large gathering of friends joined Hattie E. Wilson at her residence at 46 Carver Street on March 15 to celebrate "the attainment by their hostess of another birthday in the form."

1877–79. As "Mrs. Hattie E. Wilson," listed in *Banner of Light* as trance reader and lecturer in Room 1 of the "Hotel Kirkland" ("A family hotel," according to the Boston City Directories of the period) at Kirkland and Pleasant (now Charles Street South) streets, Boston.

1889 (September). At Boston's Paine Hall, well-known Spiritualist and reformer Moses Hull, who had nominated Frederick Douglass as vice president on the 1872 Equal Rights Party ticket, holds services after an absence of ten years spent "in the West." The *Banner of Light* lists notables in the audience, among them the Spiritualist leader "Dr. Andrew Jackson Davis" and "Dr. Hattie Wilson."[22]

1879–97. As "Mrs. Hattie E. Wilson," listed in the *Banner of Light* as trance reader and lecturer at 15 Village Street in Boston's South End; 1880 Federal Census lists her as the housekeeper of a two-family house, aged forty and a mulatto ("W" for "white" scratched out and "Mu" for "mulatto" placed over it) native of Maine; city directories of this period list her as "home, 15 Village."[23]

1897. Boston City Directories list "Mrs. Hattie E. Wilson" as "boards, 9 Pelham."[24]

1900. Hattie Wilson, residing in a boarding house at 9 Pelham Street in Boston's South End, is listed as a nurse living at the home of the Silas H. Cobb family in Quincy, Massachusetts. She falls ill in the spring of this year and is bedridden at the Cobb home at 93 Washington Street in Quincy.[25]

1900 (June 1). Federal Census enumeration for Pembroke, Plymouth County, Massachusetts, shows John G. Robinson, aged "49," born "Connecticut," occupation, "capitalist"; his "wife," Izah, aged twenty-five, born (Somerville) Massachusetts; one boarder; and a servant.[26]

1900 (June 28). "Hattie E. Wilson" dies in Quincy Hospital, Massachusetts, of "inanition"; occupation given as "nurse." Obituaries that appear in the June 29 and June 30 *Boston Herald* and *Globe,* as well as the *Quincy Daily Patriot,* state that the funeral will be held "from the residence of Mrs.

Catherine C. Cobb, 93 Washington Street, Quincy, Saturday, June 30, at 3 P.M. Train leaves South terminal station, Boston at 2:28 P.M. Relatives and friends are invited." Wilson is buried in the Cobb family plot in Mount Wollaston Cemetery in Quincy, plot number 1337, "old section."

1902 (November 7). John Gallatin "Guy" Robinson and Izah Nellie Moore, residents of Pembroke, Massachusetts, marry in Providence, Rhode Island.[27]

NOTES

1. Death certificate for Mrs. Hattie E. Wilson, giving her age as "75 years, 3 months, 13 days," dated June 29, 1900, number 192, for the City of Quincy; found in *Massachusetts Deaths* 506:95—Massachusetts Archives, Columbia Point, Boston. Names of parents, "Joshua and Margaret Green," can be found in the listing for her second marriage (*Massachusetts Marriages* 228:129). Joshua Green is also listed as Wilson's father on the death certificate.

2. 1830 Federal Census Enumeration of Population for Bedford, Hillsborough County, New Hampshire, 324. Harriet Adams may be the "white" child in the Chandler household as there is no listing for any "free colored child" in the enumeration of the population in Milford other than Timothy Blanchard's children; records indicate that "Primas [*sic*] Chandler" (1775–1859) took in pauper children. The enumerator may very well have seen Harriet and mistakenly presumed that she was white. Bedford Historical Society, *History of Bedford, New Hampshire, 1737–1971* (Somersworth, N.H.: New Hampshire Publishing Company, 1971).

3. *Our Nig*, 12–13; 14–16.

4. Information supplied by Ms. Sylvia Sebelist and Mrs. Carol Edwards, Sunbury descendants, to Reginald H. Pitts, via e-mail, March 2004.

5. *Our Nig*, 67; 1850 Federal Census for Milford, Hillsborough County, New Hampshire, sheet 166, lines 12–14.

6. Ware, Massachusetts, was possibly the "W——" that Wilson identifies as her place of refuge. R. J. Ellis suggests Worcester as

the "W——"; in the 1860s Worcester was a vibrant city with several thousand people, while Ware was no more than the "village" described in *Our Nig*. The 1850 and 1860 Federal Census Enumerations for Ware also reveal a number of people whose names mirrored those used in *Our Nig*. The candidate for "Mother" Walker is Mary Walker, a fifty-year-old English-born widow. Lewis Augustine Marsh was also teaching school at the time Wilson was in Ware; in *Our Nig*, the schoolteacher's name is Miss Marsh (Abby A. Kent). Jane Chapman Maslen Demond may have been "Allida," also called "Aunt J——"; *Our Nig*, 73. Rev. Thomas H. Jones, a fugitive slave from North Carolina, gave lectures and talks throughout southern New Hampshire and western Massachusetts raising money to free his still enslaved family. Jones passed through Milford in 1850 and most likely met Wilson at that time. See notes to the text for more information. For a compelling argument that Worcester is the more likely choice, see Barbara White, "Harriet Wilson's Mentors: The Walkers of Worcester."

7. *Farmer's Cabinet*, December 17, 1851, 1:1.

8. Ibid. Obituary for George M. Wilson, *Farmer's Cabinet*, February 29, 1860.

9. While *Our Nig* suggests that "Samuel" died in New Orleans, it is as likely that he succumbed to yellow fever in Cuba. Reviewing the crew lists of oceangoing ships that left New England ports between November 1852 and the end of June 1853, out of the nearly two hundred black sailors named Thomas Wilson, only one died—the hapless sailor on the *Cabassa*. The ship's Captain Littlejohn may have sent the news of Wilson's death from New Orleans, which was strategically located at the mouth of the Mississippi, and was a major port where ships with fresh and deepwater trade off-loaded and took on cargo. "Alphabetical List of Crews of Vessels Arriving and Departing the Port of Philadelphia, 1798–1880," 56:650. Transcribed by Pennsylvania Historical Records Survey, Harrisburg, Pennsylvania, 1937–41, Historical Society of Pennsylvania, Philadelphia. This assumes the ship stopped in Philadelphia, as so many of those with Caribbean trade routes did.

10. "Paupers Received and Discharged, 1852–1885," Hillsborough County Nursing Home (formerly Hillsborough County Farm), Goffstown, New Hampshire, as cited in White, "'Our Nig' and the She-Devil: New Information about Harriet Wilson and the 'Bellmont' Family," *American Literature* 65, no. 1 (1993), 47.

11. "Paupers Received and Discharged, 1852–1885," Hillsborough County Nursing Home (formerly Hillsborough County Farm), Goffstown, New Hampshire, as cited in White, "'Our Nig' and the She-Devil," 50. According to Joseph Carvalho III, a Harriet Wilson was enumerated in the 1855 Massachusetts State Census in the city of Springfield, living with the family of one Eli Baptiste; her age was given as twenty-five, but her birthplace was given as "Pennsylvania." The Baptiste family were natives of the area around Lancaster, Pennsylvania, and the enumerator may have assumed that the boarder in the Baptiste home was also from there. See Carvalho, *Black Families in Hampden County, Massachusetts, 1650–1855* (Westfield, Mass: Westfield State College and New England Historic Genealogical Society, 1984), 140.

12. Obituary, *Farmer's Cabinet,* February 29, 1860; 1860 Federal Census, Enumeration of Population, Death Index for Milford, Hillsborough County, New Hampshire, 12.

13. 1860 Federal Census for 2nd Ward, City of Manchester, Hillsborough County, New Hampshire, 29, shows a twenty-eight-year-old weaver named Harriet Wilson, listed as a "white" New Hampshire native living in Mrs. S. W. Young's boardinghouse.

14. White, "'Our Nig' and the She-Devil," 47.

15. All appear in the pages of the widely circulated Boston Spiritualist paper the *Banner of Light* as well as the 1850 and 1860 census returns for Milford.

16. *Banner of Light,* July 4, 18, and August 8, 1868. She is listed at 150 Tremont Street in the 1868 Boston City Directory, which collected information in October. The *Banner of Light* listings may be more accurate.

17. *Banner of Light,* 1870 Federal Census, 8th Ward of the City of Boston, sheet 15, line 4. The census has her listed at 47 Carver Street, likely a typo as multiple citations place her at 46 Carver Street.

18. *Massachusetts Marriages* 228:129, Massachusetts Archives, Columbia Point, Boston. Wilson shaves eight years off her age, making her almost ten, rather than eighteen, years older than her husband. It is not clear why Harriet E. Wilson, clearly the Milford author of *Our Nig,* is listed as white, though such mistakes were made frequently, especially as Robinson was, indeed, white, and she may have been light enough so that sometimes she was mistaken for white.

19. *Banner of Light,* April 18, 1873, 5; April 26, 1873, 5; April 11, 1874, front page.

20. *Banner of Light,* February 28, 1874, 4; June 27, 1874, 5; August 1, 1874, 4.

21. *Banner of Light,* September 5, 1874, 3; and September 26, 1874, 8; *(Chicago) Religio-Philosophical Journal,* October 10, 1874.

22. *Banner of Light,* September 21, 1889, 8.

23. 1880 Federal Census for the 1st Precinct of the 16th Ward of the City of Boston, Suffolk County Enumeration District 703, sheet 10, line 43.

24. Boston City Directory, 1897.

25. Wilson's death certificate states that the duration of her illness was two months. Silas Henry Cobb died of complications from diabetes on April 4, 1900 (Quincy Deaths for 1900, number 90; Quincy City Hall, Quincy, Mass.). If she were hired as a nurse for Silas Cobb, it would be apparent that she fell ill during the time she was taking care of him, and that the surviving Cobbs took care of her.

26. 1900 Federal Census, Town of Pembroke, Massachusetts, Plymouth County Enumeration District 1138, sheet 9, lines 86–89.

27. *Massachusetts Vital Records 1841–1910* 526:193.

Chronology II

The Hayward and Hutchinson Families of Milford, New Hampshire

1776 (January 25). Sally Hayward ("Aunt Abby") born in Maugerville, New Brunswick, Canada, daughter of Nehemiah Hayward, Sr. and Mary (Stickney) Hayward.[1]

1778 (June 13). Nehemiah Hayward, Jr. ("John Bellmont") born in Maugerville, New Brunswick, Canada.[2]

1780 (October). Rebecca S. Hutchinson ("Mrs. Bellmont," "Mrs. B.," "the 'She-Devil' ") born in Hillsborough County, New Hampshire, daughter of Nathan Hutchinson Jr. and Rebecca (Peabody) Hutchinson.[3]

1786 (March 31). Nehemiah Hayward, Sr. purchases 118 acres in the "Duxbury Mile Slip" (later a portion of the town of Milford), Hillsborough County, New Hampshire.[4]

1806 (April 29). Nehemiah Hayward, Jr. and Rebecca S. Hutchinson marry in Milford.[5]

1807 (March 9). Elizabeth "Betsy" Hayward born in Milford.[6]

1808 (August 12). George Milton Hayward ("James Bellmont") born in Milford.

1810 (April 24). Lucretia Hayward ("Jane Bellmont") born in Milford.

1813 (January 16). Nehemiah Peabody Hayward born in Milford.

1814 (August 27). Infant daughter of Haywards dies in Milford.[7]

1815 (June 23). Jonas Hutchinson Hayward ("Lewis Bellmont") born in Milford.

1818 (March 3). Charles S. Hayward ("Jack Bellmont") born in Milford. As Jack does in *Our Nig,* Charles Hayward would go west to Greenville, Illinois, with his cousin and brother-in-law Zephaniah Hutchinson in late 1839.

1820 (February 6). Infant daughter of Haywards born in Wilton, New Hampshire, dies three days later.[8]

1822 (February 3). Rebecca Smith Hayward ("Mary Bellmont") born in Milford.

1829 (April 28). David Hutchinson and Betsey Hayward marry.[9]

1831. According to *Our Nig,* six-year-old Frado (Harriet) abandoned by mother Mag (Margaret Adams or Smith) at the Hayward home in Milford.[10]

1834 (August 19). George M. Hayward ("James Bellmont") marries Nancy Abbot ("Susan Bellmont").[11]

1834 (September 9). Samuel Blanchard ("George Means") marries Lucretia Hayward ("Jane Bellmont").

1836 (March 22). Caroline Frances Hayward ("Charlie Bellmont") born to George and Nancy ("James" and "Susan").

1840 (April 7). George Milton Hayward ("James Bellmont") dies in Milford.

1840 (August 3). Rebecca S. Hayward ("Mary Bellmont") dies in Baltimore.

1841 (April 1). Charles S. Hayward ("Jack Bellmont") marries Sarah Ann Newby ("Jenny Bellmont") in Bond County, Illinois.

1847. Nehemiah Hayward, Jr. and wife Rebecca ("the Bellmonts") move to Baltimore.

1849 (May 16). Nehemiah Hayward, Jr. dies in Baltimore.

1850 (October). Rebecca Hutchinson Hayward ("Mrs. Bellmont") dies in Baltimore, of cancer.[12]

1851 (January 21). Sarah Ann Newby Hayward ("Jenny") dies in Baltimore.[13]

1857 (December 28). Charles S. Hayward ("Jack Bellmont") dies in Milford.

1859 (January 16). Sarah Hayward Blanchard ("Aunt Abby") dies in New Ipswich, New Hampshire.[14]

1859 (June 22). Lucretia Hayward Blanchard ("Jane Bellmont") dies in Clermont County, Ohio.

1860 (August 17). Nehemiah Peabody Hayward dies in Baltimore.

1863 (July 20). Betsy Hayward Hutchinson dies in Milford.

1866 (May 23). Jonas H. Hayward ("Lewis Bellmont") dies in Baltimore.

1881 (August 28). David Hutchinson (husband of Betsey Hutchinson) dies in Milford.[15]

1888 (January 6). Nancy Abbot Hayward ("Susan Bellmont") dies in Boston.

1889 (September 17). C. Frances Hayward ("Charlie Bellmont") dies in Bainbridge, Massachusetts.[16]

1900 (July 1). Samuel Blanchard ("George Means") dies in Mitchell County, Kansas, two weeks before his ninety-fifth birthday, and only three days after Hattie E. Wilson.[17]

NOTES

1. Information supplied by George H. Hayward (not a descendant) of Fredericton, Nova Scotia, to Reginald H. Pitts, via e-mail, April 1998. Hayward is a genealogist and a descendant of one George Hayward who emigrated to Maugerville, New Brunswick (then

part of Nova Scotia), about the same time as Nehemiah Hayward, Sr., though not a relative. Nehemiah emigrated with a group from Rowley, Massachusetts, led by Israel Perley and composed of various relations of the Stickney family, to which Nehemiah Hayward, Sr. was related by marriage. The governor of Nova Scotia had opened lands for settlement in Maugerville and encouraged colonists in Massachusetts and New Hampshire to emigrate with promises of cheap farmland. See Matthew A. Stickney, *The Stickney Family: A Genealogical Memoir* (Salem, Mass.: Essex Institute Press, 1869), 90, 162–64, 166–70.

2. Stickney, *Stickney Family,* 451.

3. Perley Derby, *The Hutchinson Family: Or the Descendants of Barnard Hutchinson, of Cowlan, England* (Salem, Mass.: Essex Institute Press, 1870), 36.

4. Hillsborough County Register of Deeds 16:423 (1786), Hillsborough County Court House, Nashua, New Hampshire; William P. Colburn, "Register of Milford Families," in George A. Ramsdell, *History of Milford* (Concord, N.H.: Rumford Press, 1901), 746.

5. Derby, *Hutchinson Family,* 36.

6. All information on the Hayward family found in Colburn, "Register," 746, unless otherwise noted.

7. "South-West Parish Book" for "Child of N. Haywood [*sic*]," cited in Barbara A. White, "'Our Nig' and the She-Devil: New Information about Harriet Wilson and the 'Bellmont' Family," *American Literature* 65 no. 1 (1993): 27.

8. Priscilla Hammond. *Vital Records of Wilton, New Hampshire, Compiled from the Town's Original Record Books, 1764–1848* (Concord, N.H.: Priscilla Hammond, 1936), 83.

9. Colburn, "Register," 785.

10. *Our Nig,* 12–13; 14–16.

11. Colburn, "Register," 746; Livermore and Putnam, *History of the Town of Wilton,* 546.

12. Colburn, "Register," 746; Derby, *Hutchinson Family,* 36.

13. *Baltimore Sun,* February 22, 1851.

14. White, "'Our Nig' and the She-Devil," 47.

15. Colburn, "Register," 785.

16. *Massachusetts Deaths* 345:178 for C. Frannie Hayward.

17. Information supplied by Mrs. Vickie Mears, Beloit, Kansas (descendant of Samuel Blanchard and Lucretia Hayward) to Reginald H. Pitts, June 2000.

Introduction

Liberty is our motto, Liberty is our motto,
Equal liberty is our motto, in the "Old Granite State."
We despise oppression, We despise oppression,
We despise oppression, And we cannot be enslaved.
—"The Old Granite State," The Hutchinson Family Singers

Like the glimmering spark from the meteor's fire,
Like the gay humming insects who fall and expire,
We're fading away. Fading away.
—"Fading Away," by "Hattie,"
Amherst (N.H.) *Farmer's Cabinet*, December 6, 1851

If Hattie E. Wilson, a "clairvoyant physician," diagnosed her own illness, she prescribed the right cure.[1] Once known as "our Nig" to the New Hampshire family to whom she was informally indentured as a child, Boston's "colored medium" outlived every person in whose service her health was broken. Rather than "fading away," as Hattie laments in a poem by that title published in the town paper where she grew up, she became well-known in antebellum New England and the Mid-Atlantic states for a highly successful business enterprise. Indeed, Harriet E. Wilson survived to see the twentieth century.[2] Hattie E. Wilson, as Harriet E. Wilson was called for much of her life, was ultimately overcome by the exhaustion that characterized her years in service; but she didn't succumb to this "inanition," the listed cause of her death, until she was seventy-five years old. Her friends placed announcements in Boston and Quincy papers advertising the time, location, and even the runs from South Terminal station that would bring welcome relatives and friends to celebrate her life and passing.[3] Wilson died on June 28, 1900; she is buried in Mount Wollaston Cemetery in Quincy, Massachusetts.[4]

More than forty years earlier, on September 5, 1859, Harriet E. Wilson published *Our Nig*. It tells Wilson's own story through a renamed character, a spirited six-year-old girl named Frado who is abandoned by her white mother after her "kindly African" father succumbs to consumption. As an indentured servant in the New England household of a "she-devil" "mistress" "Mrs. B," and her family, the Bellmonts, Frado is tortured and overworked for years.

Wilson is now known as one of the most important African American writers of the mid-nineteenth century. But she composed *Our Nig* when she was plagued by broken health after being freed from her indenture and deserted again, this time by her new husband, Thomas Wilson, a supposed fugitive slave, who courted—and then left—her precipitously. Faced with the confession that her husband's antislavery lectures were "a humbug for hungry abolitionists," and confronted with his inability to find legitimate local work to support them and their young son, Wilson herself turned from physical to intellectual labor. Soon after Thomas went to sea and died there, she was forced to "some experiment," as she calls *Our Nig* in its preface, "which will aid me in maintaining myself and child without extinguishing this feeble life." Wilson's "experiment" is a sophisticated hybrid of autobiography and prose fiction.

Recent research has confirmed the autobiographical claims made in *Our Nig*'s preface and appendices and has documented much of the story told within its pages. Indeed, the text so closely corresponds to the historical record that *Our Nig* lays claim to being the only extant narrative written by a black indentured servant in the antebellum North. Besides being one of the rare sketches that tells what it was like to be a poor northern-born freewoman, *Our Nig* is one of the very few narratives written by a free northern-born black at all.

Despite Wilson's signal contributions, however, her written work was ignored by her contemporaries and lost to American letters for more than 120 years. The antislavery establishment best situated to publicize *Our Nig* ignored Wilson's work. Its leaders were more interested in southern slavery than the harsh treatment blacks faced in the North; and they were no doubt offended by Wilson's critical treatment of abolitionists and spooked by her sympathetic treatment of an interracial marriage. Despite the plea of her preface to "colored brethren" for their support, they, too, overlooked Wilson's writing, perhaps because her depiction of a fake fugitive, her first husband, could do blacks of whatever status no good. Even during twentieth-century cultural movements, when a host of forgotten black narratives, novels, and treatises were resurrected, critics failed to take notice of *Our Nig*.[5] We now know that Wilson herself likely turned away from her writing and attended to her burgeoning hair product business shortly after *Our Nig*'s publication and her son's untimely death.

When Henry Louis Gates, Jr. rediscovered and republished Wilson's work in 1983, however, it enjoyed a powerful and formative twentieth-century debut. It followed hard on the heels of breakthrough bestsellers that first landed Toni Morrison on the cover of *Newsweek* and won Alice Walker a Pulitzer Prize and an American Book Award.

Once almost entirely disregarded, when Gates introduced *Our Nig* as both a newly recovered text and as the first African American women's novel, it received a warm welcome. As contemporary African American women's fiction increasingly appeared on the *New York Times* bestseller lists, Gates's rediscovery pushed back the inaugural of black women's novel writing from the early 1890s—with its host of firsts by writers such as Frances E. W. Harper and Amelia E. Johnson—to 1859.[6]

Gates's prescient argument that black reading culture was likely to have produced many more creative works by men and women than we had ever imagined proved to be right on target—despite the "pen-swords clashing over Wilson's place as first black woman novelist" that has followed.[7] The editors of Julia C. Collins's *The Curse of Caste; or The Slave Bride* (reprinted in 2006 and first serialized in the important African American newspaper the *Christian Recorder* while the Civil War drew to a close) argue that *Our Nig* is a thinly veiled autobiography. They make the case that *The Curse of Caste* is the first black woman's novel, and note that no one has yet confirmed that Gates's most recent rediscovery, *The Bondswoman's*

Narrative (written circa 1855; republished in 2002), is black-authored. At the current moment, as Rafia Zafar notes, "the identity of the first black woman novelist continues to tease us"; no critical or historical resolution seems to be in sight.

Yet, as Frances Foster suggests "the cornerstones of our reconstructed literary history" should not be contingent on a contest for primacy. Rather our touchstone texts "should be our most influential, representative, or creative texts."[8] Displaying more than its fair share of both creative and (anti-)representative qualities in its hybrid use of generic forms and conventions, *Our Nig* has become an important text in American, women's and African American letters. When read through the lens of the novelistic strategies Wilson employs, *Our Nig* complicates, as well as integrates, what Nathaniel Hawthorne dubbed the "damned mob of scribbling women," writers in the 1850s whose books sold more than a million copies and were translated into scores of languages. Susan Warner and Harriet Beecher Stowe were just two women who penned bestsellers while the writings of Herman Melville languished.

Our Nig enriches its readers' understanding of gender and of antebellum African American literary forms and messages. By the 1840s and '50s, the abolitionist movement had forged an audience for black writers who were once enslaved. As best illustrated by Frederick Douglass's 1845 publication of his life story, slave narratives—now considered a cornerstone of American literary expression—sold well. African Americans such as Douglass, William Wells Brown, and Martin Delany also began writing fiction in the 1850s, though their more overtly creative acts were less welcomed by readers than African American testimony, a seemingly simple relation of the "facts." Wilson was one of the inaugural black women able to contribute her perspective through hybrid and novelistic texts in the late 1850s. She and Frank Webb (*The Garies and Their Friends,* 1857) were among the very few who directly addressed the thorny issues of race and class in the North. This edition of *Our Nig* helps to illuminate Wilson's contribution to multiple American literary traditions and to readers' understanding of how her book engages issues of gender, geography, labor, and race.

Despite *Our Nig*'s growing popularity, until now, virtually everything beyond what Wilson's narrative chronicles has remained an unsolved mystery. This edition introduces information about Wilson's parentage, and, in doing so, raises some questions even as it answers others. By mining city directories, census records, marriage licenses, and nineteenth-century newspapers, it also offers the first full glimpse into Wilson's later life, the intriguing four decades after *Our Nig*'s 1859 publication, her son's death in 1860, and the years she spent as a "county pauper" in Hillsborough County, New Hampshire.[9] Called "Hattie," as well as "Harriet," by the mid-1860s Wilson began to use that name in public documents. Indeed, "Hattie E. Wilson" is the name used in newspaper reports of her travels as a Spiritualist lecturer; it is the name on her death certificate and gravestone.

If the age "75 years, 3 months, 13 days" given on that death certificate is correct, she was born on March 15, 1825, in Milford, New Hampshire, the daughter of Joshua and Margaret Green.[10] "My father," Wilson writes in *Our Nig*'s opening pages, worked as a "hooper of barrels" in a cooperage or barrel-making shop. Timothy Blanchard, one of the few black men in Milford, ran such a business. "Jim," as Joshua Green is called in *Our Nig,* probably met his wife, Mag, a fallen white woman, as Wilson describes her, while distributing the wood not fine enough for barrel staves but perfect to fuel the fires that kept local residents' food cooked and houses warm. According to *Our Nig,* the death of the child's father marked the waning of the family's economic health as well. Like other nineteenth-century mothers with few resources, Mag relieved herself of a child she could not support, leaving her daughter at the home of a local family whom she knew was always in need of a servant girl, though the "she-devil" lady of the house couldn't keep one "over a week" because of her "ugly" disposition (12).

The poignancy of "our Nig" 's situation stems not only from her abandonment, but also from the service to which she was consigned after her mother left her. When a newspaper printed the suggestion that women should take up the "light work and kind appreciation" found in domestic service, New Hampshire abolitionist Parker Pillsbury offered a much-needed corrective: "the work is never 'comparatively light' in genteel households," he retorted. "Never."[11] Sleeping in alternately stifling and freezing quarters, being overworked to the point of exhaustion, and enduring depressing isolation were the norms in service.[12] As a young black child indentured to a white family in a town that only a handful of blacks called home, Wilson experienced a fate even worse than the typical northern indenture. For much of her childhood at the home of Nehemiah Hayward, Jr. and his wife, Rebecca (Hutchinson) Hayward, she was probably the only female "free colored person" in all of Milford.[13] Moreover, girls who were "bound out" were seldom as young, and, though isolated, they were rarely cut off completely from their families, which provided a source of both solace and protection.[14] Wilson's assertion that slavery casts shadows even in the North sets up an apt comparison between the experiences she describes and the life of an enslaved youngster separated from kin and community.

The personal claim made in the opening chapter title, "Mag Smith, My Mother," could be more literal even than readers once thought.[15] Indeed, if "Margaret Ann Smith," a twenty-seven-year-old New Hampshire woman who died in Boston, corresponds to the "lonely Mag Smith" whose story *Our Nig* first recounts, then soon after she left Milford, Harriet's mother died in much the same way that she had lived. After her husband's death, Mag (as nineteenth-century Margarets were often called), descends into a "darkness," casually taking on one of her husband's partners as a lover, and engaging in tense domestic scenes that became "familiar and trying" (11). Before the couple decides to relieve themselves of her child and leave town to find work, Mag is "morose and revengeful" (6), and subject to "fits of desperation" and "bursts of anger" (11). Margaret Ann Smith, and the black man with whom she resided, seemed to have lived in much the same way.

The March 27, 1830, *Farmer's Cabinet*—the paper that covered the area in which Wilson grew up—reports Smith's death in detail:

> Margaret Ann Smith, black, late of Portsmouth N.H. about 27 years was found dead in the room of a black man with whom she lived in Southack [*sic*] Street, Boston, last week. The verdict of

> the Coroner's jury was that she came to her death from habitual intoxication. It appears that she and the man had quarreled, both being intoxicated, and he had beaten her severely, but that the immediate cause of her death was drinking half a pint of raw rum.—*Patriot.*

Though the *Boston Patriot* mentions a death from intemperance, it does not report the details of Margaret Smith's untimely—and unseemly—demise. However, the news was salacious enough to appear in multiple other papers in New Hampshire and Massachusetts. Indeed, the *Farmer's Cabinet* reprinted the notice word for word from the Portsmouth, New Hampshire, *Journal of Literature & Politics,* where it ran earlier that week. The story appeared in areas where *Our Nig*'s Mag Smith and this Margaret Smith seem to have lived. Paying close attention to the reprint provenance also reveals that in several other papers, the deceased had *no* racial assignation. Margaret Ann Smith, it turns out, like *Our Nig*'s Mag Smith, was not black after all. In its time line and its details, then, the *Cabinet* article corresponds to the story *Our Nig* tells. Mag was not born in "Singleton," as Milford is called in the book; she relocated there. Then, after passing "into an insensibility" no taunts could penetrate (13), and that read very much like "familiar and trying" scenes (12) and signs of alcoholism, she leaves with her black lover around 1830.[16]

The newspaper accounts raise intriguing questions. Why does Margaret (Mag) Smith suddenly appear as black in later printings that announce her death? Does the *Cabinet* reprint this version because they choose to make a subtle point about her social and sexually compromised status, her intimate connections with black men? How does this resonate with Wilson's challenging play with her readers' racialized expectations in *Our Nig,* as she chooses not to reveal Mag's racial designation—she could very well be a light-skinned black woman—until the very last paragraph of the chapter that tells her story? And what do we make of the last names that are associated with Wilson and her parents in the public record? Her father's name was most certainly Joshua Green; her mother's name was, indeed, Margaret. But Harriet never lists her mother's maiden name on later records. She also uses the surname Adams in the early 1850s (until she marries Thomas Wilson in 1851), not Green or Smith. After Mag's "will made her the wife of Seth" (11), did the family become known by her paramour's name? Did Harriet's biological parents never legally marry? Or did Harriet, ever attuned to the symbolic power of naming, adopt a new name, as so many narrators do, to mark the end of servitude?[17]

In the first chapter title, the author claims "Mag Smith" as "My Mother" in a text otherwise told almost entirely in the third person. Likewise, Wilson claims this story, *Our Nig* by "our Nig," as her own.[18] And although neither the importance nor the authenticity of the text depends on its claim to truth—as shifting, situated, and ultimately unrecoverable as any narrative truth claims are—new evidence both broadens and bolsters literary historian Barbara A. White's point that the "lives of the Haywards," into whose family the young Harriet was indentured, "correspond so closely to the narrative . . . as to remind us that Henry Louis Gates, Jr. [the book's first editor], not Harriet Wilson, classifies *Our Nig* as fiction."[19]

From the beginning to the end and with very few exceptions, Wilson's narrative corresponds to the historical record. If "Mag Smith" is "Margaret Ann Smith," she moved southwest from Portsmouth, New Hampshire, to Milford, leaving "the few friends she possessed," to "seek an asylum among strangers" (5). In *Our Nig,* "Jim" "boards cheap" with the cooper who employs him, and the 1820 and 1830 censuses show that Timothy Blanchard ("Pete Greene"), the cooperage owner, and one of Milford's two black heads of households, boarded other "free men of color," one of whom was almost certainly Wilson's father Joshua Green.[20] Indeed, one of Timothy Blanchard's nieces could easily have been the other "little colored girl," the "favorite playmate," who went missing with Frado after she overheard she was to be given away, (12–13).[21] Moreover, as White has established, the portrayal of the "County Home" found in *Our Nig* corresponds almost exactly to descriptions and town records for the support of the poor.[22]

Our Nig's story overlaps with the closing testimonials that function to authenticate its claims and, again, new evidence confirms the details both *Our Nig* and its appended documents recount. Indeed, before the woman who would later christen herself Madame C. J. Walker was born in the last days of 1867, Wilson's hair care products were widely advertised throughout the entire Northeast.[23] Freed from her indenture and faced with poverty and poor health, as *Our Nig* reports, a friend provided Frado with "a valuable recipe" that restored "gray hair to its former color." Availing "herself of this great help [she] has been quite successful," "Allida" reports in an appended document, "but her health is again failing, and she has felt herself obliged to resort to another method of procuring her bread—that of writing an Autobiography."[24] We now know that as early as 1857, Wilson sold "hair dressing" and "hair regenerator" in a business that would eventually be based in Manchester, New Hampshire. The bottles still exist. Tens of thousands were certainly sold.[25]

Harriet Wilson refers to *Our Nig* as "sketches" or "narrations," while the author of one of the closing testimonials, as we've seen, urges others to buy the "interesting work" she calls an "autobiography" (76). Yet this narrative, as Priscilla Wald points out, "is not finally just an autobiography"; it is a sociopolitical allegory and a "narrative *about* autobiography."[26] Even as we recover the direct correspondences between Wilson's text and her life, we might do well to heed Guilia Fabi's caution that the appreciation of the literariness of early African American and women's writing is often overshadowed by the emphasis on the sociohistorical context.[27] The census records, newspaper citings, city directory listings, and marriage and death certificates that confirm the "facts" described in *Our Nig* and that legitimize the book's autobiographical claims are not meant to *bind* the narrative to the historical record, to become yet another authenticating apparatus. Literary forms and generic lines are fluid. *Our Nig* is prototypical of black antebellum writing in its tendency to blend and challenge the narrative forms it incorporates, weaving together factual and fictional conventions. Indeed, *Our Nig* functions as an autobiography characterized by its complex novelistic maneuvers just as surely as one can argue that it is a brilliant novel that makes autobiographical claims.

While critics often emphasize the ways in which *Our Nig* weaves together the conventions of sentimental fiction and slave narratives, it also includes strong references to a variety of popular genres, including the seduction novel and the captivity narrative. Gates has outlined how vividly the text aligns itself with (and revises) the generic strategies of the sentimental novel.[28] Yet *Our Nig* also emphatically rejects many aspects of domestic ideology: the redeeming power of motherhood and the ability of marriage to bring either happiness or stability to women or children, for example. As Amy Lang contends, in domestic fiction as the protagonist "exchanges rage for patience, the terms of her identity shift from poor to female, and she is awarded a home. Once gender is established as the source of social mobility and the guarantor of social harmony, the narrative focus shifts from social justice to individual reform, from deprivation to self-control."[29] The racism documented in *Our Nig* makes it impossible for Frado to join or claim a family or fulfill the maternal and material expectations of womanhood valued by sentimental ideology. *Our Nig* challenges domestic ideals that privilege bourgeois home maintenance without providing a point of entry for those who have been excluded, at least as mistresses of their own homes. In that way, *Our Nig* can be characterized as *anti*-sentimental; it offers perhaps the strongest and most subversive challenge to sentimental ideology and literary conventions articulated in antebellum women's fiction.

Our Nig's opening incorporates the language and conventions of the seduction novel, an eighteenth-century form that includes runaway bestsellers like Samuel Richardson's *Pamela* (1740) and Susannah Rowson's *Charlotte Temple* (1791), books that remained enormously popular throughout the next century. *Our Nig* ingeniously merges Mag's tale of sexual seduction with Frado's story of service by recalling *Pamela,* the British novel named for a servant girl pursued by her employer, the wealthy "Mr. B.," who attempts to forcibly seduce the eponymous heroine he holds captive at his estate before recognizing her virtue and marrying her. *Our Nig*'s Mrs. Bellmont, "Mrs. B.," recalls

Pamela's antagonist. The British Mr. B.'s attempt to "ruin" and "undo" his servant girl informs the American Mrs. B.'s attempt to ruin her own. In *Our Nig,* however, sex and marriage are not ultimately items of exchange that hold transformative power. *Our Nig* instead highlights the connection between control of one's own labor and one's own body; it underscores the harm done by the quotidian physical violence meted out—and tolerated—by white women and men, and by extension, by the North, when the abused party is black and economically vulnerable.

Our Nig's tone, if not its language, is pitched in economically deterministic registers. Economic desire, the wish to "ascend to [her seducer] and become an equal" (5), motivates Mag to surrender a "gem," her virtue, then to marry a black man ("want" is a "powerful philosopher and preacher" [9]), and subsequently to abandon her child. Financial hardship likewise is the reason for Wilson's separation from her own young son, who, until his death six months after *Our Nig*'s publication, alternately resided with his mother when she could afford it, in the Hillsborough County Poor Farm in Goffstown in which he was born, and was boarded out at others' homes. When Frado first arrives at the Bellmonts', the youngest daughter, the devilish Mary, says, "Send her to the County House," "in reply to the query what should be done with her" (15). Mary's words—or Wilson's rendition of them—prove prophetic. Wilson's child ends up in the home of others, as Frado was, separated from his mother. Thus, while much has been made of *Our Nig*'s sentimentality, with its rhetorical arc, dark narrative resolution, and depiction of mothers incapable of transcending their poverty, Wilson's writing anticipates the grim determinism of twentieth-century novels by Richard Wright and Ann Petry as much as it echoes the sentiments expressed in the writings of Wilson's contemporaries Harriet Beecher Stowe, Susan Warner, and Maria Cummins.

By stressing the permanence, scope, and violence of her servitude—"slavery's shadows"—Wilson implies that the racially neutral category of northern indenture is inadequate in explaining the circumstances and experiences she describes. The physical torture that Frado endures while no one is held accountable either in private or public spheres, the recurring runaway plot, and the possessive qualities in black chattel labor implied by the family's moniker "our Nig"—all of these themes tie the text to another popular form, the life stories published by and about former slaves. The continuous references to Mrs. B.'s racialized sense of the totality and permanence of her ownership rights to "her" servant's body and soul, signal that indenture is not an appropriate model through which to understand Frado's experience. Instead, through the subliterary rendition of her story, Wilson levels a devastating critique of northern race relations.

But, importantly, neither Wilson nor Frado is enslaved. And so we might consider how *Our Nig* draws on another popular early American form, the captivity narrative. This genre, which had enormous currency in the eighteenth century, was generally associated with innocent captives, often women, held by so-called savage American Indians. Although critics conventionally refer to the life stories penned by Solomon Northup, Harriet Jacobs, and Lucy A. Delaney as slave narratives, the books relate how the authors, their mothers, or their grandmothers, were illegally robbed of the freedom to which they were entitled. *Our Nig* can be usefully grouped with these narratives; all claim not only that blacks are unjustly enslaved as a class under existing laws, but also that they are free individuals who have been unjustly held captive by the illegal subversion of those laws. Originating in New England, where Mary Rowlandson—whose book is often cited as the first and most influential of the genre—was abducted, many of these narratives share *Our Nig*'s geographical terrain. Wilson remaps the genre's racial assumptions about victimization and virtue; in *Our Nig* white women are savage villains, while a racial outsider, here a young black girl, is held captive in New England.

While the Haywards (the "Bellmonts"), the family that held young Harriet, no doubt justified the hard labor, poor diet, harsh domestic conditions, and physical treatment she endured in terms of her indenture, to this date there have been no documents found that confirm that they registered or formalized her service. *Our Nig*'s publication closely followed an 1857 act of the New Hampshire state legislature that provided "that no person should be deprived of the right of citizenship in the state on account of color, or because that person had been a slave." Any person "found guilty of this felony was to be confined to hard labor not less than one, nor more than five, years."[30] In this context, *Our Nig*'s literary indictment may have carried the weight of legal conviction as well as moral indignation, even though the principals in *Our Nig* had almost all died by that time. Critics generally agree that one motivation for Wilson's using fictional names might be her fear of reprisal from the living Hayward relatives. This, too, underscores *Our Nig*'s indictment of slavery's appurtenances North, as she puts it in her preface. Several writers who were once enslaved—most notably Harriet Jacobs, who called herself Linda Brent—renamed the principals in their narratives for fear that their testimony would provoke a backlash.

While New Hampshire was a state proud of its patriotic commitment to freedom, it had not always been as welcoming to citizens or visitors of color as the passage of the 1857 act implies. In 1835, in the U.S. Congress, New Hampshire Senator Isaac Hill justified mob violence against black students, their white counterparts, and the abolitionists who had invited them all to Canaan, New Hampshire, to study at the multiracial Noyes Academy. Hill explained that local residents stood against abolitionist schemes to mingle the races. Using rhetoric that could characterize the twentieth as well as the nineteenth century, the town's reaction to an integrated school, he suggested, reflected their fears that an influx of blacks would overrun Canaan, inviting poor people who would tax the town's resources and subject its citizens to public nuisances.

The actions Canaan residents took to avoid such nuisances culminated in New Hampshire's ugliest historical episode concerning black education. Occurring when Wilson was about ten, this episode in Canaan eerily frames *Our Nig*'s description of Frado's first days in school: being teased by her classmates and spurned by the young Mary Bellmont, who enjoyed tormenting Frado in private and shunned the thought of "walking with a nigger" in public (18). Henry Highland Garnet and Alexander Crummell, who would become intellectual giants of the nineteenth-century antislavery and black rights movements, and Anglo American Richard Rust, who would later found the Freedmen's Aid Society and Rust College, faced far worse. They were young men when they joined twelve blacks and twenty-seven young whites of both sexes at the newly founded academy. Though abolitionists were sanguine about the town's reception, opposing residents made their patriotic wishes known on July 4, when the ensuing mob had to be dispersed by a local magistrate.

In a town meeting, a committee organized to do away with the school in "the *interest* of the town, the *honor* of the State, and the *good* of the whole community."[31] On August 10, Canaan whites rallied neighbors and, with nearly a hundred yoke of oxen, pulled the school from its foundation, dragging it into a swamp half a mile away. Young people like Julia Ward Williams and her future husband, Garnet, who had traveled four hundred miles to study there, were not to have "the opportunity to show that they are capable, equally with the whites, of improving themselves in every scientific attainment, every social virtue, and every Christian ornament," as the young people and the Noyes founders had hoped.[32] Instead, Garnet and eleven other black students had to face down a violent assault on their boardinghouse with shotguns and then, with Garnet sick and no doubt terrified, they had to flee the town while the mob fired a cannon as their wagon retreated.[33] In 1835, ninety miles north of Milford, Noyes's students were confronted with public expressions of racial violence. By that same year, Frado's experience in public school—one of the few places where "she had rest from Mrs. Bellmont's tyranny"—had ended. Mrs. Bellmont felt that Frado's "time and person belonged solely to her" (24). Using the language of ownership to claim Frado as her private property, Mrs. Bellmont reined the young girl back into "her place," a black girl's proper place, that is, in the domestic and racial order.

A host of staunch New Hampshire abolitionists and reformers condemned public violence against blacks and their supporters, and even more residents of the Granite State, as they called New Hampshire, opposed slavery, however ambivalent they were in their feelings toward free blacks like Wilson. They thought themselves worthy of the poet John Greenleaf Whittier's paean to "New Hampshire" in his poem by the same name. Inspired by Senator John P. Hale, who broke the infamous gag rule by openly condemning slavery on the floor of the U.S. Congress, Whittier imagined the Granite State's antislavery credentials to be rock solid. Ending with the lines "Courage, then, Northern hearts! Be firm, be true; / What one brave State hath done, can ye not also do?" the poem joined the Hutchinson Family Singers' "The Old Granite State" (which they sang for President Tyler at the White House in 1844) as one of the most famous anthems to celebrate antebellum New Hampshire.

Although Frederick Douglass would praise the Milford-based Hutchinson Family Singers for having "sung the yokes from the necks and the fetters from the limbs of my race," Harriet Wilson was not impressed.[34] The ties between the well-loved and renowned Hutchinson family and the Haywards must have been particularly hard for the young Wilson to stomach or understand. Betsey, one of the "Bellmont" children "already settled in homes of their own" (14), married the eldest Hutchinson son, David, in 1829. The couple stayed close by, and their families' lives were intertwined in multiple ways. Frado's favorite, "Jack Bellmont," or Charles Hayward, did indeed go West, as *Our Nig* outlines. He was accompanied by his brother-in-law Zephaniah Hutchinson, who had once been the manager for his siblings, the famous singers.[35] When the Hutchinson Singers visited Baltimore, as Barbara White has established, they stayed with Jonas Hayward (Lewis Bellmont), who made their arrangements and took them to visit the grave of his sister, Rebecca, Frado's nemesis "Mary."[36]

The Hutchinson Singers were known as not just "performers," as the most famous antislavery newspaper put it, "but abolitionists."[37] And they brought the news of their travels home. In 1842, for example, when George Latimer was captured and imprisoned in Boston, Jesse and John Hutchinson—both members of the famous singing group—joined a group of some fifty men who "were resolved to make an effort towards rescuing" the fugitive. Soon they were "at the head of the delegation," marching to the famous Marlboro Chapel, singing, "Oh, liberate the bondsman." In a letter in which John reports their success, he closes by saying "after the Latimer incident Sister Abby and I returned to Milford." Linked to the antislavery front line in this way and others, the town was no isolated outpost in the struggle for abolition. If it is "distinguished for anything," said a speaker at Milford's Centennial Celebration, "it is for the unselfish and sublime work of these splendid men and women in the grandest movement of the century, for human rights."[38]

Little good it did Wilson that New Hampshire was the home of several prominent abolitionists. The radical Stephen S. Foster had helped to organize the New Hampshire Young Men's Anti-Slavery Society just a year after Noyes Academy was demolished—and he stayed active and uncompromising for decades—but this did nothing to alleviate Wilson's condition in a "two-story white house, North" as she put it in *Our Nig*'s subtitle.[39] Milford's Leonard Chase was one of the three New Hampshire subscription agents for the widely circulated paper the *Liberator,* and the vice president of the state's antislavery society.[40] His home at 15 High Street, Milford, was a stop on the underground railroad. And Horace Greeley, the nationally prominent editor of the *New York Tribune,* hailed from nearby Amherst, New Hampshire. Indeed, the Reverend Humphrey Moore had married Nehemiah and Rebecca Hayward, the "Bellmonts," before he was elected to the state legislature in 1840 and 1841, where he "gave stirring orations against slavery."[41]

Local reformers' brave and active roles in civil disobedience in New Hampshire, Boston, and elsewhere raises questions about the town residents' passivity toward the practically enslaved girl growing up in their midst. Placing *Our Nig* in the antislavery context of its time personalizes a central human contradiction and a particularly American paradox: how can people who stand firmly against injustice ignore it—or enact it—in their own front yards?

The discontinuity between Milford's public face and young Harriet's private life helps to explain the sardonic tone that seethes just beneath the narrative's surface. She must have experienced the swell of antislavery activity in Milford as she reached her majority, or was about to turn eighteen, as if antislavery reformers were dancing on top of her living grave. Abolitionist meetings and challenges to Northern churches led up to, and followed, the huge abolitionist rally the town hosted in 1843. Reformers braved snow and wind to hear the eloquent George Johnson and George Latimer, whose case prompted the largest acts of civil disobedience in the nineteenth century, speak about their captivity. They also heard from Pillsbury, Foster, and Nathaniel Rogers, the editor of New Hampshire's *Herald for Freedom*. At least one historian claims that William Lloyd Garrison, the movement's greatest editor; Frederick Douglass, its most powerful writer and witness; Wendell Phillips, its most eminent orator; and the most important national and state reformers swelled the town's numbers on a "granite winter" day when Wilson was in her teens.[42] During that decade Garrison visited again. And Douglass reported in his paper, the *North Star*, that he met a "good anti-slavery friend" and gave four "real old-fashioned meetings, full of life and spirit" in Milford in 1848.[43] In Wilson's experience, however, white abolitionists not only in her area, but throughout New England, "didn't want slaves at the South, nor niggers in their own houses, North. Faugh! to lodge one; to eat with one; to admit one through the front door; to sit next to one; awful!"(71).

Our Nig's last lines, "Frado had passed from their memories as Joseph from the butler's, but she will never cease to track them till beyond mortal vision" (72), offer conventional narrative resolution appropriate to the genres from which Wilson draws. Quoted from the Bible, they are comforting and gender appropriate. Wilson reports that many of Frado's would-be supporters have found their way to heaven. Her words are also empowering. Frado has outlived Mrs. B. and recounted her agonizing death. She has bested her foes and has wrested from them the control she lacked as a child. *She* tracks *them*. They cannot escape her, even though they are dead and gone. Prophetically, in the end, it is Wilson's writing that determined how they are remembered in the twentieth and twenty-first centuries.

The reference to Joseph, an enslaved seer and interpreter of dreams who was abandoned, indeed sold, by his family, and forgotten by those whom he once had helped, also anticipates Wilson's growing connection to Spiritualism, which was sweeping the country in the 1840s and 1850s. It was a major, nearly ubiquitous, nineteenth-century movement that appropriated space for women's expression and leadership in religious, political, social, and medical reform. The movement was an heir of mid-century religious awakenings that would spawn Christian Science, Seventh Day Adventism, Mormonism, Mesmerism, and the Oneida, New Harmony, and Northampton communities, among others. Like those who believed in phrenology and biometrics, Spiritualism's adherents, who held that spirits' messages were conducted through electricity, linked it to scientific progress and the surge of discoveries that were then changing the way society understood both natural phenomena and itself.

In their lecture halls, conventions, and camp meetings, Spiritualists discussed the larger concerns of women, labor, and racial oppression. Before the Civil War, the movement was popular with many leading abolitionists. After 1865, they took up the cause of the eight-hour workday, women's rights in marriage and childbearing, and Indian removal. Clairvoyant physicians challenged draconian practices—the overprescribing of toxic doses of purgatives, stimulants, and narcotics such as opium and mercury—and rejected the medical establishment's restrictions on women because of their supposed inclination toward "hysteria." Instead, they relied on homeopathic remedies.[44] Though in the present day, nineteenth-century Spiritualism is commonly associated with séances, spirit communication, the "planchette" and Ouija board, and often dismissed as mere quackery, it was one of the most important, and radical, movements of its time. Its adherents included the familiar names of journalist Horace Greeley, historian George Bancroft, abolitionists and women's rights activists Sarah and Angelina Grimké, Sojourner Truth, Elizabeth Cady Stanton, and William Lloyd Garrison, among others. To that pantheon, we can now add Hattie E. Wilson.

After daring to write a book that lays claim to being both the first black woman's novel and an important autobiography of an indentured servant, Wilson continued to challenge convention and to exceed the expectations of those who thought little of her capabilities. Months after her son's death, and just a year after she published *Our Nig,* Wilson made a stunning turnaround. As Katherine Flynn has discovered, modest advertisements for "Mrs. Wilson's Hair Regenerator," "believed to be the best preoration [sic] for the hair ever made," appeared in Wilson's local paper, the *Farmer's Cabinet,* for more than a year and a half—beginning in the fall of 1857. Indeed, as Wilson ends *Our Nig* she describes how she was "busily employed in preparing her merchandise; then sallying forth to encounter many frowns, but some kind friends and purchasers" (72). She suspended these efforts during the fifteen months during which she applied for *Our Nig*'s copyright and as her son became ill and passed away. A little more than six months after his death, however, advertisements for "Mrs. H. E. Wilson's Hair Dressing" and "Hair Regenerator" were running in newspapers in five states—from New Jersey to Maine. By 1861, Wilson's products were being sold by local agents in multiple cities, and half-column-long advertisements were appearing in at least seven states accompanied by customer testimonials. Ads warned buyers to "be careful and obtain Mrs. H. E. Wilson's Hair Dressing, as the name will be blown in every bottle, and you can obtain it in almost every store in the United States or Canada." The recipe Wilson refers to in the closing pages of *Our Nig* proved to be valuable indeed. By using it to launch this hair care venture, she became an important foremother not only in black women's literature but also in black women's entrepreneurial history.[45]

By 1867, Wilson had left New Hampshire and was living in East Cambridge, Massachusetts, appearing on platforms with Spiritualist leaders such as Andrew Jackson Davis, one of the most important authors, speakers, and philosophers of the movement, and Pascal Beverly Randolph, one of the few black mediums of national renown. Known as "the earnest colored trance medium," Wilson gave fervent addresses in Boston on labor reform and children's education.[46] At a camp meeting in

Melrose, Massachusetts, where three thousand people gathered, Wilson's speech "excited thrilling interest and was at once an eloquent plea for the recognition of her race [and] the sentiment and philosophy of universal brotherhood."[47] By 1868, she was advertising her services as a lecturer and trance physician and was doing well enough to make generous financial contributions to Spiritualist conventions.[48]

In Boston, she joined forces with a young apothecary, John Gallatin Robinson. Soon after, though he was white and eighteen years her junior, she married him. Their marriage certificate shows that Harriet E. Wilson, born in Milford, New Hampshire, but residing in Boston, daughter of Margaret and Joshua Green, was entering into her second marriage. She is listed, erroneously, and perhaps euphemistically, as thirty-seven years old (if she was born in 1825, she would have actually been forty-five). She is also listed in public records of that time as white, though she was widely known as Boston's "colored medium."[49] In the oft-noted feminist spirit of the movement, she again bucked custom, alternately calling herself both by her married name, Hattie E. Robinson, and by the name by which we continue to know her, Hattie E. Wilson.

Like Achsah Sprague, who recovered from a debilitating illness to become one of the mid-nineteenth century's most famous mediums and lecturers, when Hattie E. Wilson became a Spiritualist, she found it a life-changing as well as life-saving experience. As she described it to her peers on a fall morning in 1870, one day "she had been brought into acquaintance with her father in spirit-life." At first she was opposed to becoming a medium, she reports, but was finally convinced by "seeing an old schoolmate who had been dead several years standing by her bedside, who conversed with her as naturally as ever. Then her father came and gave all the facts of his life and acquaintance with her mother, manifesting the tenderest interest in her."[50] Wilson's experience follows the path to spiritualism taken by countless men and women attracted to the growing movement when faced with the loss of loved ones. Abolitionist reformers Amy and Isaac Post, New York Supreme Court judge John W. Edmonds, *New York Tribune* editor Horace Greeley and his wife, and First Lady Mary Todd Lincoln, for example, all became associated with spiritualism after the death of a child.

When John Robinson wed Hattie Wilson, he married a woman whose name and products had appeared in thousands of newspapers and advertisements. She was also becoming an increasingly popular lecturer in the Spiritualist community. Wilson found enthusiastic audiences throughout the Northeast, not only in Massachusetts, but in Connecticut, Maine, and New Hampshire as well. Reports of her successful addresses were sometimes printed in the Spiritualist press.[51] In 1873, she reportedly shared the platform with Victoria Woodhull, who had run for president on the Equal Rights Party ticket in the previous year, and had just recently emerged from one of the most scandalous libel trials of the century. Sixteen thousand assembled to hear the speakers, including Hattie E. Wilson.[52] Wilson traveled as far as Chicago as a delegate to the American Association of Spiritualists. At the Universal Association of Spiritualists, reported as "a mass meeting of Radicals and Reformers," by one paper and a "mongrel convention" by another, she delivered an oration of "great vigor" on the "conduct of Spiritualists to each other, founded on personal experience" and also challenged "the doctrine of turning children over to the state."[53] She joined a community that worked to establish children's lyceums, Spiritualist Sunday schools, and sang in quartets at meetings.

Even the social gatherings Wilson organized were covered in the *Banner of Light,* a Spiritualist paper that claimed subscribers in every state and territory.[54] When, on February 13, 1874, the anniversary of her son George's death, she gave "an anniversary in honor of her spirit father," it was "attended by a goodly number of friends" who gathered at her home on 46 Carver Street before adjourning to a hall where prominent Boston Spiritualists made appropriate remarks. Dancing went on until midnight. And on March 15, 1876, when Wilson organized a gathering at her house, "a large gathering of her friends" came out to celebrate "the attainment by their hostess of another birthday."[55]

Almost a decade earlier, in 1867, at least some of the former stalwarts of the New England abolitionist community had taken note of Hattie Wilson. William Cooper Nell corresponded regularly with Amy Post, a Rochester, New York, abolitionist, reformer, and Spiritualist who was the close friend of Harriet Jacobs, author of *Incidents in the Life of a Slave Girl* (1861). Nell, a black activist and historian who spearheaded successful efforts to integrate Boston's public schools, wrote to Post about their shared interests and social circles. An avowed Spiritualist, he reported that he "found but little opportunity to attend the New England Convention or the Spiritualists Meeting—and knew nothing of the Colored Medium Mrs. Wilson. It may be some one of my acquaintances."[56] Early in her career, then, Wilson drew the attention of at least one important black Boston reformer whose connections included a wide range of former abolitionists and black activists who were still laboring on the political and social issues of their day. One wonders about the relationship that Wilson and Nell may have established, as they were two of the few black Spiritualists in Boston, and Nell's wife, Frances, whom he would marry in 1869, was from Nashua, New Hampshire (some ten miles from Milford), where Wilson once lived.[57]

Still active as a lecturer and trance reader, by 1879 Wilson was settled as the housekeeper of a two-family home at 15 Village Street in Boston's South End. She was to stay there for eighteen years. In 1889, when Moses Hull, the famous Spiritualist and reformer who once nominated Frederick Douglass to the Equal Rights Party ticket as vice-president, appeared in Boston after a nearly ten-year hiatus, the newspaper *Banner of Light* announced the notable Spiritualists who were in the audience. Andrew Jackson Davis and "Dr. Hattie Wilson" were among them. By this time, Hattie and John Gallatin Robinson had probably gone their separate ways. Spiritualists believed that marriage was an institution that too often oppressed women and that the bonds of spiritual love rather than the dicta of the state should guide couples' decisions. By 1900, Robinson was living with Izah Moore, his twenty-five-year-old wife, according to the census. He would marry her in 1902, two years after Wilson—his legal wife—had died.

In 1900, Wilson left her beloved Boston and went to live with, and perhaps work for, the family of Silas and Catherine Cobb in nearby Quincy. Perhaps she was employed as a nurse—the occupation listed on her death certificate—or perhaps the Cobbs were friends. Whatever the case, Silas Cobb passed away in April. Wilson fell ill later that month, and after a sickness of two months died in Quincy Hospital of "inanition" or exhaustion. Unlike the Haywards, the Cobb family clearly valued its relationship with Hattie E. Wilson. She is buried in their family plot; her name is engraved on a massive and impressive Quincy granite headstone alongside theirs.

As a child, Wilson had been scoffed at for her attempts to find spiritual comfort and reproached by her mistress for turning into a "pious nigger" who might expect to "preach to white folks" (49). As a mature and emancipated woman, she did just that. After a short-lived but stunning entrepreneurial venture, Wilson spent the last thirty-five years of her life as a "lecturer," "trance reader," and "clairvoyant physician." She joined the luminaries of a movement that took issues of labor reform, women's rights, and spirituality—and took Hattie Wilson herself—seriously. The record shows that, as in *Our Nig*, Wilson continued to speak about her condition and experiences, offering sometimes trenchant and often humorous commentary that "excited thrilling interest" and was "an eloquent plea for the recognition of her race."

—P. GABRIELLE FOREMAN

The editors wish to extend their deepest appreciation to Katherine Flynn for her collaboration in unearthing the scope of Mrs. H. E. Wilson's hair product enterprise. Thanks to Denise Burgher for her work in identifying Wilson's biblical references. Thanks to Rhondda Thomas, Suzanne Schneider, Andrea Williams, and Elena Abbott for their companionship, research assistance, and collaboration. Thanks also to Alan Lewis, Bill Neal, Julie Winch, Charlotte Edwards, and Priscilla Wald for their intellectual generosity.

NOTES

1. The 1870 Federal Census and the Boston city directories of the period list her as "Dr. Hattie E. Wilson." It was not unusual for nineteenth-century citizens to call themselves medical practitioners on the basis of their readings on the subject, says critic John Ernest. William Wells Brown, whose novel *Clotel* (1853), published in London, launched the black novelistic tradition, started adding M.D. to his name in 1864 or 1865, calling himself a "dermapathic and practical physician." John Ernest, *Resistance and Reformation in Nineteenth-Century African-American Literature* (Jackson: University of Mississippi Press), 215 n. 1.

2. *Farmer's Cabinet,* December 6, 1851.

3. *Boston Herald,* obituary announcements, June 29 and 30, 1900. *Boston Globe,* obituaries, June 29, 1900. The service was held at 8:00 P.M. on June 30.

4. Death certificate for Hattie E. Wilson, giving her age as "75 years, 3 months, 13 days," dated June 29, 1900, number 192, for the City of Quincy, found in *Massachusetts Deaths* 506:95, Massachusetts Archives, Columbia Point, Boston, Massachusetts. Hattie E. Wilson was born in Milford, New Hampshire to Joshua Green. The "maiden name and birthplace of mother" line is left blank.

5. In the late 1960s and early 1970s, civil rights movements impacted publishing and curricular changes. Arno Press and the Negro University Presses, for example, reissued hosts of important black books that had been out of print. Women's novels by authors such as Nella Larsen, Jessie Fauset, Gwendolyn Brooks, and Ann Petry were again in circulation. Many of these novels were out of print again by the late 1970s, only to be resurrected ten years later.

6. Frances E. W. Harper's "Two Offers," serialized in the first editions of the *Anglo-African,* is known as the first short story by a black woman. Maria F. dos Reis published a novel called *Ursula* in Brazil in 1859.

7. Zafar, "Of Print and Primogeniture, or, the Curse of Firsts," 620.

8. Foster, "Forgotten Manuscripts: How Do You Solve a Problem Like Theresa?" *African American Review* 40.4 (Winter 2006): 632.

9. Barbara White, John Ernest, R. J. Ellis, and Eric Gardner have built considerably on Henry Louis Gates, Jr.'s groundbreaking research.

White established the historical identities of the family members in whose service Wilson spent her childhood. R. J. Ellis's cultural biography of *Our Nig,* which came out as this edition was in progress, does path-clearing work on New Hampshire and Milford abolition. Eric Gardner's primary research traces the publishing and circulation history of *Our Nig*'s first edition. Ellis notes that "after 1856 we know nothing for sure about Harriet Wilson except that *Our Nig* is entered in her name in Boston in 1859 and that her son died in 1860." R. J. Ellis, *Harriet Wilson's "Our Nig": A Cultural Biography of a "Two-Story" African American Novel* (Amsterdam: Rodopi, 2003), 29. In his 2002 reprint edition, Gates states that "researchers, including Barbara A. White, have found no trace of Wilson after 1863." Gates, ed., *Our Nig,* lxxxiv.

10. See both her death certificate (*Massachusetts Deaths* 506:25) and her second marriage certificate (*Massachusetts Marriages* 228:129), which lists both her parents' names (Joshua and Margaret Green) and her Milford birthplace. In the most thorough historical work done to that date, Barbara White pointed out that spring 1825 would be a likely time for Wilson's birth "because all of the age markers in *Our Nig* are given in the Spring." See "'*Our Nig* and the She-Devil': New Information about Harriet Wilson and the 'Bellmont' Family," *American Literature* 65, no. 1 (1993): 41.

11. See Faye E. Dudden, *Serving Women: Household Service in Nineteenth-Century America* (Middletown, Conn.: Wesleyan University Press, 1983), 195.

12. Dudden, *Serving Women,* 196–97, 225.

13. According to the 1840 census, when Harriet would have been about fifteen, there were no other female "free colored persons" in Milford.

14. "Orphaned children were commonly bound out at about age ten or twelve to serve until they were eighteen." Dudden, *Serving Women,* 20. R. J. Ellis, citing Joan M. Jensen, *With These Hands: Women Working the Land* (New York: Talman, 1980), disagrees, suggesting that seven was a typical age for mid-Atlantic farm women (Ellis, *Harriet Wilson's "Our Nig,"* 105). For comparisons and commentary on indenture by enslaved blacks, see Douglass, *Narrative of the Life,* in which he compares his servitude to the indenture of his shipyard friends. Also see Moses Roper, *A Narrative of the Adventures and Escape of Moses Roper, from American Slavery,* in *North Carolina Slave Narratives,* ed.

William Andrews et al. (Chapel Hill: North Carolina University Press, 2003), 28.

15. This recalls Harriet Jacobs's use of Amy and Isaac Post's real names in *Incidents in the Life of a Slave Girl*, a narrative in which all other principals are renamed. Henry Louis Gates, Jr.'s findings definitively establish that Wilson went by Harriet Adams before her marriage to Thomas Wilson in 1851. Harriet Adams appears on the document recording her first marriage and on the 1850 census records that establish she was living with the family of Samuel Boyles that year. R. J. Ellis speculates that Adams might not be Harriet's mother's married name, "but instead her maiden name (or even a name invented for Harriet)." See Ellis, *Harriet Wilson's "Our Nig,"* 35. Wilson's second marriage and death certificates confirm his suspicion. They both list Wilson's birthplace as Milford, New Hampshire, and her father's name as Joshua Green. Again, both parents, as Margaret and Joshua Green, appear on the marriage license. The death certificate leaves blank the line that identifies her mother. Why she would use the name Adams if her maiden name was Green and her parents were, as we assume, married, is still an open question.

16. The *Farmer's Cabinet,* March 27, 1830, 1. The exact notice appears in the Portsmouth, New Hampshire, *Journal of Literature & Politics* of March 25, 1830. It seems to be reprinted from another Portsmouth paper, the *New Hampshire Gazette* of March 23, 1830, which attributes its source (mistakenly) as the "Boston Pat." The *Eastern Argus Semi-Weekly* printed the story in their March 19, 1830, issue, citing the source of the article in full as the "*Boston Palladium,*" whose official name was the *New-England Palladium and Commercial Advertiser*. This newspaper provenance clears up why the *Farmer's Cabinet* attributed the notice to a paper (the *Patriot*—presumably, the *Boston Patriot* and the *New England Patriot*) that does not cover the notice of her death in such detail.

17. Frado would have just turned five if both her death certificate and this account are correct. *Our Nig* states that she is abandoned when she is six. Wilson's birth year, even taking into account the exactness of the death certificate, still begs for verification. Census records and her own creative accounting, on her second marriage certificate, for example, complicate any definitive answer to that question. The 1830 notice of Margaret Smith's death closely correlates to Wilson's childhood recollections. See Foreman, *Activist Sentiments,* 57–70.

18. See Henry Louis Gates, Jr.'s introduction to the 1983 edition for a reading of the inverted commas Wilson uses "to underscore [her] use as an ironic one, one intended to reverse the power relation implicit in renaming-rituals." She renames herself not our Nig but "our Nig," as Gates points out (introduction, li).

19. White, "New Information about *Our Nig*," 23, 29, and 44. There are at least three self-consciously substantial ways in which *Our Nig* diverges from the historical record. "Aunt Abby" or Sally Hayward Blanchard, who in the narrative appears as a "maiden aunt," was widowed, a fact that Wilson more than likely knew. And *Our Nig* excises, or merges into another brother, a rendering of Nehemiah Peabody Hayward, probably, as critics have suggested, for the sake of narrative flow that would be disrupted with an ungainly number of principal characters. Caroline Frances, the daughter of George and Nancy Hayward ("James and Susan Bellmont"), also appears as a boy, Charlie Bellmont, in *Our Nig*.

20. The 1820 census shows that in addition to Blanchard, two other free colored males lived at his residence. The 1830 census indicates that one black man, between ten and twenty-four, was housed there. Blanchard had brothers, but they were all older than he. He was thirty-nine in 1830, the year, presumably, in which Joshua Green succumbed to consumption.

21. Sara Malysa, the eldest daughter of Timothy and Dorcas Hood, his (white) wife, was born in Milford on July 16, 1830, and so is probably too young to be Frado's favorite playmate. Her sister, Elizabeth, was born on September 6, 1834. They had Salem cousins (Cecilia and Sarah Coleman, born in 1823 and 1827), and their mother and Timothy's other sisters remained closely connected to the Milford family. When Timothy died in 1839, his sister Sarah and her husband, William Coleman, would take the Blanchard girls to Salem, where they and other relatives shared in the girls' care and were active in the African American community. Sara and Elizabeth would grow up to marry African Americans from Salem. Their older brothers, George Walter (1824–96) and Tim Blanchard, Jr. (1828–?), were both enumerated in the 1850 census for Milford as living with their maternal grandfather, Joseph Hood; George would be listed as white in public records until his death in 1896. The youngest two, James and Henry, who was barely a toddler, however, ended up in the Milford poorhouse. Henry was eventually apprenticed to a black barber, William Henry Montague, of Springfield, Massachusetts, where he would

stay until 1864. And James worked on farms in nearby Amherst, where he is listed in both the 1850 and 1860 censuses, until he joined the (white) 10th New Hampshire Infantry. Dorcas Hood remarried Luther Elliot, a white property owner. When James, whom she evidently abandoned to the poorhouse, died during the Civil War, she would collect his pension. See Pension Records for Mrs. Dorcas H. Elliot, mother of Private James Blanchard, Company H, 10th New Hampshire Infantry Regiment, National Archives; Death Certificate for Mrs. Sara M. (Blanchard) Washington, dated July 9, 1910, Massachusetts State Archives, Columbia Point, Boston, Massachusetts. See William P. Colburn, "Register," in George A. Ramsdell, *The History of Milford, with Family Registers* (Concord, N.H.: 1901), 593; and White, "New Information about *Our Nig,*" 48 n. 12, for information on the Blanchard boys' time in the poorhouse. Also see Reginald H. Pitts, "George and Timothy Blanchard: Surviving and Thriving in Nineteenth-Century Milford."

22. See White, "New Information about *Our Nig,*" 24.

23. Sarah Breedlove McWilliams Walker (1867–1919), born in Delta, Louisiana, on the banks of the Mississippi River, was known professionally as Madame C. J. Walker. She worked as a laundress and dressmaker who developed a conditioning treatment to straighten hair, which she first sold door-to-door. By advertising her products and teaching others to treat hair, she became the first African American female millionaire. See A'Lelia Perry Bundles, *On Her Own Ground: The Life and Times of Madame C. J. Walker* (New York: Charles Scribner's Sons, 2001).

24. Letter by "Allida," appendix to *Our Nig,* 76.

25. Wilson writes of the "valuable recipe" from which she found a "useful article for her maintenance" (72); and "Allida" gives more details (76). The bottles were produced by Henry Wilson & Co. and Tewksbury & Wilson of Manchester. In 1856, Henry Wilson was a clerk at 22 Elm Street, Manchester. The same year, Monroe G. J. Tewksbury was a physician at 37 Elm Street. By 1858, the two were together as Tewksbury & Wilson, Apothecaries, 45 Elm Street, and were again listed together in 1860. In 1861, Henry Wilson buys the Lion Drug Store in the central Merchant Exchange building in Manchester and is soon not only advertising but manufacturing "Mrs. Wilson's Hair Dressing and Hair Regenerator." See, for example, Wilson's "Union Almanac" for Hillsborough and Rockingham Counties and the State of New

Hampshire, Henry P. Wilson, issuer, Gage and Farnsworth Printers, Manchester, 1862. After suffering from ill health in 1862, reports Kathy Flynn, he fails to appear in the *Manchester Directory* after 1864, the year in which he loses both his daughter and wife to disease. He moves south, later returns to New Hampshire and remarries, and lives until 1918. Report from Kathy Flynn to Gabrielle Foreman, October 8, 2008. Also see *Manchester City Directory* (Boston: Sampson & Murdock, 1871). See Foreman and Flynn, "Mrs. H. E. Wilson, Mogul?" *Boston Globe,* February 15, 2009; Ideas section.

26. Priscilla Wald, *Constituting Amerians: Cultural Anxiety and Narrative Form* (Durham, N.C.: Duke University Press, 1995), 169.

27. M. Guilia Fabi, *Passing and the Rise of the African American Novel* (Urbana: University of Illinois Press, 2001), 1.

28. See Gates, introduction to *Our Nig* (New York: Vintage, 2002), xli–liv. See also Ellis, *Harriet Wilson's "Our Nig,"* chapter 3.

29. Amy Lang, "Class and the Strategies of Sympathy," in *The Culture of Sentiment: Race, Gender, and Sentimentality in Nineteenth Century America,* ed. Shirley Samuels (New York: Oxford University Press, 1992), 130.

30. J. W. Hammonds, "Slavery in New Hampshire," *Magazine of American History with Notes and Queries* 21 (January–June, 1889): 65.

31. Douglas Harper, "Slavery in New Hampshire," www.slavenorth.com/newhampshire.htm.

32. Harper, "Slavery in New Hampshire."

33. Sterling Stuckey, "A Last Stern Struggle: Henry Highland Garnet and Liberation Theory," in *Black Leaders of the Nineteenth Century,* ed. Leon Litwack and August Meier (Urbana: University of Illinois Press, 1988), 132. Garnet and Crummell later attended Oneida Institute in New York.

34. Douglass also wrote the introduction to Jonas Hutchinson's *Story of the Hutchinsons.* See White, "New Information on *Our Nig,*" 51 n. 35. Carol Brink, *Harps in the Wind: The Story of the Singing Hutchinsons* (New York: MacMillan, 1947), 286.

35. See "Explanatory Notes," p. 91, for more information. Also see White, "New Information on *Our Nig,*" 35.

36. White, "New Information on *Our Nig,*" 37.

37. *Liberator,* January 20, 1843, 2.

38. Ramsdell, *History of Milford,* 522.

39. Joshua Hutchinson writes that in 1874 he was living "on Amherst Street, Milford, N.H., the former residence of Parker Pillsbury." *A Brief Narrative of the Hutchinson Family* (Boston: Lee and Shepard, 1874), 66.

40. Chase represented the area in the state legislature in 1850 and 1851. Ramsdell, *History of Milford,* 433.

41. White, "New Information on *Our Nig,*" 27.

42. Nathaniel Rogers writes of his travels with Parker Pillsbury to the Milford meeting in the *Herald of Freedom,* January 13, 1843. He writes that the "weather tried even [Pillsbury's] hardihood of endurance" and that "anti-slavery service has touched his manly shoulders and they can't bear granite winters as they used to." The convention is also covered in the *Liberator,* January 20, 1843, 2. See Brink, *Harps in the Wind,* 55, for the most impressive account; while it may be true that all of these luminaries attended, neither the *Liberator* nor the *Herald of Freedom* mention Douglass, Garrison, Remond, or Phillips. Though Brink quotes their resolutions in detail, she provides no sources. She or her own sources may have confused the Boston Female Anti-Slavery Society meeting advertised in the *Liberator* on January 27, 1843, 3, with the Milford meeting. Foster chaired the Milford meeting. Jesse Hutchinson, the brother who lived in Lynn, Massachusetts, and the other siblings were there, and made a definite impression on those who wrote the *Liberator* notice.

43. *North Star,* June 9, 1848, 2.

44. See Ann Braude, *Radical Spirits: Spiritualism and Women's Rights in Nineteenth-Century America* (Bloomington: Indiana University Press, 2001), 142–61.

45. See Foreman and Flynn, "Mrs. H. E. Wilson, Mogul?"

46. *Banner of Light,* June 15, 1867, 3. See also July 6, 1867, 8.

47. *Banner of Light,* September 14, 1867, 5.

48. *Banner of Light,* June 27, 1868, 3; July 18, 1868, 8.

49. "Hattie E. Wilson" is listed as white in the 1870 census and on her second marriage certificate. She is, nonetheless, the same "Hattie E. Wilson, colored," who appears in *Banner of Light* monthly list-

ings for years. Indeed the addresses on the census record match the *Banner*'s listings. The 1880 census lists her as white (W) which is then crossed out and "Mu" for mulatto is scribbled over it. Wilson's death certificate lists her color as "African," and, as we have seen, confirms that she was born in Milford, and that her father's name is Joshua Green.

50. *Banner of Light,* November 12, 1870, 2.

51. *Banner of Light,* October 19, 1867, 5; November 28, 1867, 8; January 4 and December 5, 1868, for example.

52. *Banner of Light,* August 23, 1873. The listing of Hattie C. Robinson is almost surely a typographical error. She is listed throughout the year as Hattie E. Robinson and Hattie E. Wilson; no other Hattie Robinson, or Hattie C. Robinson, appears.

53. *Banner of Light,* September 26, 1874, 8. See also the *Religio-Philosophical Journal,* Vol. 17–18, October 10, 1874, 6.

54. Braude, *Radical Spirits,* 29.

55. *Banner of Light,* February 28, 1874, 4; *Banner of Light,* March 25, 1876, 4.

56. Letter from Nell to Post, Boston, June 23, 1867, in *William Cooper Nell: Selected Writings, 1832–1874,* ed. Dorothy Porter Wesley and Constance Porter Uzelac (Baltimore: Black Classics Press, 2002), 670. Nell would die in 1874.

57. Frances A. Ames's mother was Lucy Drake Ames; her father was Phillip O. Ames, a black barber, whom, considering Wilson's hairdressing business in Nashua, Wilson very well may have known. Frances would return to Nashua with her two young sons but would return by 1880 to Boston. Porter, ed., *William Cooper Nell,* 48.

Suggestions for Further Reading

ARTICLES AND CHAPTERS IN COLLECTIONS

Andrews, William L. "A Poetics of Afro-American Autobiography," in *Afro American Literary Studies in the 1990s*, Houston Baker and Patricia Redmond, eds. Chicago: University of Chicago, 78–97.

——— "The Novelization of American Voice in Early African American Narrative," *PMLA* 105 (January 1990): 23–36.

Bassard, Katherine Clay. "Beyond Mortal Vision: Harriet Wilson's *Our Nig* and the American Racial Dream-Text" in *Female Subjects in Black and White Race, Psychoanalysis, Feminism*," Elizabeth Abel, Barbara Christian, and Helene Moglen, eds. Berkeley: University of California Press, 1997.

Breau, Elizabeth. "Identifying Satire: *Our Nig*" *Callaloo*, 16.2 (1993).

Christian, Barbara. "Somebody Forgot to Tell Somebody Something: Black Women's Historical Novels" in *Wild Women in the Whirlwind: Afra-American Culture and the Contemporary Literary Renaissance*, ed. Joanne Braxton and Andree McLaughlin. New Brunswick, N.J.: Rutgers University Press, 1990.

Davis, Cynthia J. "Speaking the Body's Pain: Harriet Wilson's *Our Nig*," *African-American Review* 27.3 (1993): 391–404.

Foreman, P. Gabrielle. "Recovered Autobiographies and the Marketplace: *Our Nig*'s Generic Genealogies and Harriet Wilson's Entrepreneurial Enterprise" in *Harriet Wilson's New England: Race, Writing, and Region*, eds. Boggis, Raimon, and White, Lebanon, N.H.: University of New Hampshire Press, 2007: 123–38.

Foreman, P. Gabrielle, and Katherine Flynn. "Mrs. H. E. Wilson, Moul?" *Boston Globe* (February 15, 2009), Ideas section.

Foster, Frances Smith. "Forgotten Manuscripts: How Do You Solve a Problem Like Theresa?" *African American Review* 40.4 (Winter 2006): 631–45.

Fox-Genovese, Elizabeth. "My Statue, My Self: Autobiographical Writings of Afro-American Women," in *Reading Black, Reading Feminist: A Critical Anthology,* ed. Henry Louis Gates, Jr. New York: Meridian, 1990, 176–203.

Gardner, Eric. "This Attempt of Their Sister: Harriet Wilson's *Our Nig* from Printer to Readers." *New England Quarterly* 66.2 (June 1993): 226–46.

———. "Of Bottles and Books: Reconsidering the Readers of Harriet Wilson's *Our Nig*" in *Harriet Wilson's New England: Race, Writing, and Region,* eds. Boggis, Raimon, and White. Lebanon, N.H.: University of New Hampshire Press, 2007: 3–26.

Gates, Henry Louis Jr. "Introduction." *Our Nig*. New York: Vintage Books, 1983.

Holloway, Karla F. C. "Economies of Space: Markets and Marketability in *Our Nig* and *Iola Leroy,*" in *The (Other) American Traditions: Nineteenth-Century Women Writers,* ed. Joyce W. Warren. New Brunswick, N.J.: Rutgers University Press, 1993, 126–140.

Jackson, Cassandra. "Beyond the Page: Rape and the Failure of Genre" in *Harriet Wilson's New England: Race, Writing, and Region,* eds. Boggis, Raimon, and White. Lebanon, N.H.: University of New Hampshire Press, 2007: 155–66.

Johnson, Ronna C. "Said but Not Spoken: Elision and the Representation of Rape, Race and Gender in Harriet E. Wilson's *Our Nig,*" in *Speaking the Other Self: American Women Writers*. Athens: University of Georgia Press, 1997, 96–115.

Leveen, Lois. "Dwelling in the House of Oppression: The Spacial, Racial, and Textual Dynamics of Harriet Wilson's *Our Nig.*" *African American Review* 35.4 (2001): 561–80.

Mullen, Harryette. "Runaway Tongue: Resistant Orality in *Uncle Tom's Cabin, Our Nig, Incidents in the Life of a Slave Girl* and *Beloved,*" in *The Culture of Sentiment: Race, Gender, and Sentimentality in Nineteenth-Century America,* ed. Shirley Samuels. New York: Oxford University Press, 1992, 244–64.

Peterson, Carla L. "Capitalism, Black (under) Development, and the Production of the African American Novel in the 1850s." *American Literary History* 4 (1992).

Pitts, Reginald H. "George and Timothy Blanchard: Surviving and Thriving in Nineteenth-Century Milford," in *Harriet Wilson's New England: Race, Writing, and Region,* eds. Boggis, Raimon, and White. Lebanon, N.H.: University of New Hampshire Press, 2007: 41–66.

Pratofiorito, Ellen. "'To Demand Your Sympathy and Aid': *Our Nig* and the Problem of No Audience." *Journal of American and Comparative Cultures* 24.1 (2001): 31–48.

Stern, Julia. "Excavating Genre in *Our Nig.*" *American Literature* 67.3 (1995): 439–66.

West, Elizabeth J. "Reworking the Conversion Narrative: Race and Christianity in *Our Nig.*" *Melus* 24.2 (1999): 3–27.

White, Barbara A. "'*Our Nig*' and the She-Devil: New Information about Harriet Wilson and the 'Bellmont' Family." *American Literature* 65.1 (1993): 19–52.

———. "Harriet Wilson's Mentors: The Walkers of Worcester," in *Harriet Wilson's New England: Race, Writing, and Region,* eds. Boggis, Raimon, and White, Lebanon, N.H.: University of New Hampshire Press, 2007: 27–40.

Yarborough, Richard. "The First Person in Afro-American Fiction," in *Afro American Literary Studies in the 1990s,* eds. Houston Baker and Patricia Redmond. Chicago: University of Chicago, 1989, 105–21.

Zafar, Rafia. "Of Print and Primogeniture, or, the Curse of Firsts," *African American Review* 40.4 (Winter 2006): 619–21.

BOOKS

Andrews, William. *To Tell a Free Story: The First Century of Afro-American Autobiography, 1760–1865.* Urbana: University of Illinois Press, 1986.

Boggis, Jerri Anne, Eve A. Raimon, and Barbara A. White, eds. *Harriet Wilson's New England: Race, Writing, and Region.* Lebanon, N.H.: University of New Hampshire Press, 2007.

du Cille, Ann. *The Coupling Convention: Sex, Text and Tradition in Black Women's Fiction.* New York: Oxford University Press, 1993.

Ellis, R. J. *Harriet Wilson's "Our Nig:" A Cultural Biography of a "Two-Story" African American Novel.* Amsterdam: Rodopi Press, 2003.

Ernest, John. *Resistance and Reformation in Nineteenth-Century African-American Literature.* Jackson: University of Mississippi Press, 1995.

Foreman, P. Gabrielle. *Activist Sentiments: Reading Black Women in the Nineteenth Century.* Urbana: University of Illinois Press, 2009.

Foster, Frances Smith. *Written By Herself: Literary Production by African American Women, 1746–1892.* Bloomington: Indiana University Press, 1993.

Gates, Henry Louis, Jr. *Figures in Black: Words, Signs and the "Racial" Self.* New York: Oxford University Press, 1987.

Melish, Joanne Pope. *Disowning Slavery: Gradual Emancipation and Race in New England, 1780–1860* (Ithaca, N.Y.: Cornell University Press, 1998).

Peterson, Carla L. *Doers of the Word: African American Women Speakers and Writers in the North (1830–1880).* New York: Oxford University Press, 1995.

Raimon, Eve Allegra. *The "Tragic Mulatta" Revisited: Race and Nationalism in Nineteenth Century Antislavery Literature.* Piscataway, N.J.: Rutgers University Press, 2004.

Reid-Pharr, Robert F. *Conjugal Union: The Body, the House and the Black American.* New York: Oxford University Press, 1999.

Santamarina, Xiomara. *Belabored Professions: Narratives of African American Working Womanhood.* Chapel Hill: University of North Carolina Press, 2005.

Tate, Claudia. *Domestic Allegories of Political Desire: The Black Heroine's Text at the Turn of the Century.* New York: Oxford University Press, 1992.

Wald, Priscilla. *Constituting Americans: Cultural Anxiety and Narrative Form.* Durham, N.C.: Duke University Press, 1995.

Zafar, Rafia. *We Wear the Mask: African Americans Write American Literature, 1760–1870.* New York: Columbia University Press, 1997.

A Note on the Text

The text of this edition follows the original 1859 edition published by Geo. C. Rand & Avery in Boston, Massachusetts.

OUR NIG;

OR,

Sketches from the Life of a Free Black,[1]

IN A TWO-STORY WHITE HOUSE, NORTH[2]

SHOWING THAT SLAVERY'S SHADOWS FALL EVEN THERE.

BY "OUR NIG."

"I know
That care has iron crowns for many brows;
That Calvaries are everywhere, whereon
Virtue is crucified, and nails and spears
Draw guiltless blood; that sorrow sits and drinks
At sweetest hearts, till all their life is dry;
That gentle spirits on the rack of pain
Grow faint or fierce, and pray and curse by turns;
That hell's temptations, clad in heavenly guise
And armed with might, lie evermore in wait
Along life's path, giving assault to all."—HOLLAND.[3]

BOSTON:
PRINTED BY GEO. C. RAND. & AVERY[4]
1859

PREFACE.

In offering to the public the following pages, the writer confesses her inability to minister to the refined and cultivated, the pleasure supplied by abler pens. It is not for such these crude narrations appear. Deserted by kindred, disabled by failing health, I am forced to some experiment which shall aid me in maintaining myself and child[5] without extinguishing this feeble life. I would not from these motives even palliate slavery at the South, by disclosures of its appurtenances North. My mistress was wholly imbued with *southern* principles. I do not pretend to divulge every transaction in my own life, which the unprejudiced would declare unfavorable in comparison with treatment of legal bondmen; I have purposely omitted what would most provoke shame in our good anti-slavery friends at home.[6]

My humble position and frank confession of errors[7] will, I hope, shield me from severe criticism. Indeed, defects are so apparent it requires no skilful hand to expose them.

I sincerely appeal to my colored brethren[8] universally for patronage, hoping they will not condemn this attempt of their sister to be erudite, but rally around me a faithful band of supporters and defenders.

H. E. W.

CHAPTER I.

MAG SMITH, MY MOTHER.[1]

Oh, Grief beyond all other griefs, when fate
First leaves the young heart lone and desolate
In the wide world, without that only tie
For which it loved to live or feared to die;
Lorn as the hung-up lute, that ne'er hath spoken
Since the sad day its master chord was broken!

MOORE[2]

Lonely Mag Smith! See her as she walks with downcast eyes and heavy heart. It was not always thus. She *had* a loving, trusting heart. Early deprived of parental guardianship, far removed from relatives, she was left to guide her tiny boat over life's surges alone and inexperienced. As she merged into womanhood, unprotected, uncherished, uncared for, there fell on her ear the music of love, awakening an intensity of emotion long dormant. It whispered of an elevation before unaspired to; of ease and plenty her simple heart had never dreamed of as hers. She knew the voice of her charmer, so ravishing, sounded far above her. It seemed like an angel's, alluring her upward and onward. She thought she could ascend to him and become an equal. She surrendered to him a priceless gem, which he proudly garnered as a trophy, with those of other victims, and left her to her fate.[3] The world seemed full of hateful deceivers and crushing arrogance. Conscious that the great bond of union to her former companions was severed, that the disdain of others would be insupportable, she determined to leave the few friends she possessed, and seek an asylum among strangers. Her offspring came unwelcomed, and before its nativity numbered weeks, it passed from earth, ascending to a purer and better life.

"God be thanked," ejaculated Mag, as she saw its breathing cease; "no one can taunt *her* with my ruin."

Blessed release! may we all respond. How many pure, innocent children not only inherit a wicked heart of their own, claiming life-long scrutiny and restraint, but are heirs also of parental disgrace and calumny, from which only long years of patient endurance in paths of rectitude can disencumber them.

Mag's new home was soon contaminated by the publicity of her fall; she had a feeling of degradation oppressing her; but she resolved to be circumspect, and try to regain in a measure what she had lost. Then some foul tongue would jest of her shame, and averted looks and cold greetings disheartened her. She saw she could not bury in forgetfulness her misdeed, so she resolved to leave her home and seek another in the place she at first fled from.

Alas, how fearful are we to be first in extending a helping hand to those who stagger in the mires of infamy; to speak the first words of hope and warning to those emerging into the sunlight of morality! Who can tell what numbers, advancing just far enough to hear a cold welcome and join in the reserved converse of professed reformers, disappointed, disheartened, have chosen to dwell in unclean places, rather than encounter these "holier-than-thou" of the great brotherhood of man!

Such was Mag's experience; and disdaining to ask favor or friendship from a sneering world, she resolved to shut herself up in a hovel she had often passed in better days, and which she knew to be untenanted. She vowed to ask no favors of familiar faces; to die neglected and forgotten before she would be dependent on any. Removed from the village, she was seldom seen except as upon your introduction, gentle reader, with downcast visage, returning her work to her employer, and thus providing herself with the means of subsistence. In two years many hands craved the same avocation; foreigners who cheapened toil and clamored for a livelihood, competed with her, and she could not thus sustain herself. She was now above no drudgery. Occasionally old acquaintances called to be favored with help of some kind, which she was glad to bestow for the sake of the money it would bring her; but the association with them was such a painful reminder of by-gones, she returned to her hut morose and revengeful, refusing all offers of a better home than she possessed. Thus she lived for years, hugging her wrongs, but making no effort to escape. She had never known plenty, scarcely competency; but the present was beyond comparison with those innocent years when the coronet of virtue was hers.

Every year her melancholy increased, her means diminished. At last no one seemed to notice her, save a kind-hearted African, who often called to inquire after her health and to see if she needed any fuel, he having the responsibility of furnishing that article, and she in return mending or making garments.

"How much you earn dis week, Mag?" asked he one Saturday evening.

"Little enough, Jim.[4] Two or three days without any dinner. I washed for the Reeds,[5] and did a small job for Mrs. Bellmont;[6] that's all. I shall starve soon, unless I can get more to do. Folks seem as afraid to come here as if they expected to get some awful disease. I don't believe there is a person in the world but would be glad to have me dead and out of the way."

"No, no, Mag! don't talk so. You shan't starve so long as I have barrels to hoop. Peter Greene[7] boards me cheap. I'll help you, if nobody else will."

A tear stood in Mag's faded eye. "I'm glad," she said, with a softer tone than before, "if there is *one* who isn't glad to see me suffer. I b'lieve all Singleton[8] wants to see me punished, and feel as if they could tell when I've been punished long enough. It's a long day ahead they'll set it, I reckon."

After the usual supply of fuel was prepared, Jim returned home. Full of pity for Mag, he set about devising measures for her relief. "By golly!" said he to himself one day—for he had become so absorbed in Mag's interest that he had fallen into a habit of musing aloud—"By golly! I wish she'd *marry* me."

"Who?" shouted Pete Greene, suddenly starting from an unobserved corner of the rude shop.

"Where you come from, you sly nigger!" exclaimed Jim.

"Come, tell me, who is't?" said Pete; "Mag Smith, you want to marry?"

"Git out, Pete! and when you come in dis shop again, let a nigger know it. Don't steal in like a thief."

Pity and love know little severance. One attends the other. Jim acknowledged the presence of the former, and his efforts in Mag's behalf told also of a finer principle.

This sudden expedient which he had unintentionally disclosed, roused his thinking and inventive powers to study upon the best method of introducing the subject to Mag.

He belted his barrels, with many a scheme revolving in his mind, none of which quite satisfied him, or seemed, on the whole, expedient. He thought of the pleasing contrast between her fair face and his own dark skin; the smooth, straight hair, which he had once, in expression of pity, kindly stroked on her now wrinkled but once fair brow. There was a tempest gathering in his heart, and at last, to ease his pent-up passion, he exclaimed aloud, "By golly!" Recollecting his former exposure, he glanced around to see if Pete was in hearing again. Satisfied on this point, he continued: "She'd be as much of a prize to me as she'd fall short of coming up to the mark with white folks. I don't care for past things. I've done things 'fore now I's 'shamed of. She's good enough for me, any how."

One more glance about the premises to be sure Pete was away.

The next Saturday night brought Jim to the hovel again. The cold was fast coming to tarry its apportioned time. Mag was nearly despairing of meeting its rigor.

"How's the wood, Mag?" asked Jim.

"All gone; and no more to cut, any how," was the reply.

"Too bad!" Jim said. His truthful reply would have been, I'm glad.

"Anything to eat in the house?" continued he.

"No," replied Mag.

"Too bad!" again, orally, with the same *inward* gratulation as before.

"Well, Mag," said Jim, after a short pause, "you's down low enough. I don't see but I've got to take care of ye. 'Sposin' we marry!"

Mag raised her eyes, full of amazement, and uttered a sonorous "What?"

Jim felt abashed for a moment. He knew well what were her objections.

"You's had trial of white folks, any how. They run off and left ye, and now none of 'em come near ye to see if you's dead or alive. I's black outside, I know, but I's got a white heart inside.[9] Which you rather have, a black heart in a white skin, or a white heart in a black one?"

"Oh, dear!" sighed Mag; "Nobody on earth cares for *me*—"

"I do," interrupted Jim.

"I can do but two things," said she, "beg my living, or get it from you."

"Take me, Mag. I can give you a better home than this, and not let you suffer so."

He prevailed; they married. You can philosophize, gentle reader, upon the impropriety of such unions, and preach dozens of sermons on the evils of amalgamation.[10] Want is a more powerful philosopher and preacher. Poor Mag. She has sundered another bond which held her to her fellows. She has descended another step down the ladder of infamy.

CHAPTER II.

MY FATHER'S DEATH.[1]

Misery! we have known each other,
Like a sister and a brother,
Living in the same lone home
Many years—we must live some
Hours or ages yet to come.

SHELLEY.[2]

Jim, proud of his treasure,—a white wife,—tried hard to fulfil his promises; and furnished her with a more comfortable dwelling, diet, and apparel. It was comparatively a comfortable winter she passed after her marriage. When Jim could work, all went on well. Industrious, and fond of Mag, he was determined she should not regret her union to him. Time levied an additional charge upon him, in the form of two pretty mulattos, whose infantile pranks amply repaid the additional toil. A few years, and a severe cough and pain in his side compelled him to be an idler for weeks together, and Mag had thus a reminder of by-gones. She cared for him only as a means to subserve her own comfort; yet she nursed him faithfully and true to marriage vows till death released her. He became the victim of consumption.[3] He loved Mag to the last. So long as life continued, he stifled his sensibility to pain, and toiled for her sustenance long after he was able to do so.

A few expressive wishes for her welfare; a hope of better days for her; an anxiety lest they should not all go to the "good place;" brief advice about their children; a hope expressed that Mag would not be neglected as she used to be; the manifestation of Christian patience;[4] these were *all* the legacy of miserable Mag. A feeling of cold desolation came over her, as she turned from the grave of one who had been truly faithful to her.

She was now expelled from companionship with white people;

this last step—her union with a black—was the climax of repulsion.

Seth Shipley,[5] a partner in Jim's business, wished her to remain in her present home; but she declined, and returned to her hovel again, with obstacles threefold more insurmountable than before. Seth accompanied her, giving her a weekly allowance which furnished most of the food necessary for the four inmates. After a time, work failed; their means were reduced.

How Mag toiled and suffered, yielding to fits of desperation, bursts of anger, and uttering curses too fearful to repeat. When both were supplied with work, they prospered; if idle, they were hungry together. In this way their interests became united; they planned for the future together. Mag had lived an outcast for years. She had ceased to feel the gushings of penitence; she had crushed the sharp agonies of an awakened conscience. She had no longings for a purer heart, a better life. Far easier to descend lower. She entered the darkness of perpetual infamy. She asked not the rite of civilization or Christianity. Her will made her the wife of Seth. Soon followed scenes familiar and trying.

"It's no use," said Seth one day; "we must give the children away, and try to get work in some other place."

"Who'll take the black devils?" snarled Mag.

"They're none of mine," said Seth; "what you growling about?"

"Nobody will want any thing of mine, or yours either," she replied.

"We'll make 'em, p'r'aps," he said. "There's Frado's six years old, and pretty, if she is yours, and white folks'll say so. She'd be a prize somewhere," he continued, tipping his chair back against the wall, and placing his feet upon the rounds, as if he had much more to say when in the right position.

Frado, as they called one of Mag's children, was a beautiful mulatto, with long, curly black hair, and handsome, roguish eyes, sparkling with an exuberance of spirit almost beyond restraint.

Hearing her name mentioned, she looked up from her play, to see what Seth had to say of her.

"Wouldn't the Bellmonts[6] take her?" asked Seth.

"Bellmonts?" shouted Mag. "His wife is a right she-devil! and if—"

"Hadn't they better be all together?" interrupted Seth, reminding her of a like epithet used in reference to her little ones.

Without seeming to notice him, she continued, "She can't keep a girl in the house over a week; and Mr. Bellmont wants to hire a boy to work for him, but he can't find one that will live in the house with her; she's so ugly, they can't."

"Well, we've got to make a move soon," answered Seth; "if you go with me, we shall go right off. Had you rather spare the other one?" asked Seth, after a short pause.

"One's as bad as t'other," replied Mag. "Frado is such a wild, frolicky thing, and means to do jest as she's a mind to; she won't go if she don't want to. I don't want to tell her she is to be given away."

"I will," said Seth. "Come here, Frado?"

The child seemed to have some dim foreshadowing of evil, and declined.

"Come here," he continued; "I want to tell you something."

She came reluctantly. He took her hand and said: "We're going to move, by-'m-bye; will you go?"

"No!" screamed she; and giving a sudden jerk which destroyed Seth's equilibrium, left him sprawling on the floor, while she escaped through the open door.

"She's a hard one," said Seth, brushing his patched coat sleeve. "I'd risk her at Bellmont's."

They discussed the expediency of a speedy departure. Seth would first seek employment, and then return for Mag. They would take with them what they could carry, and leave the rest with Pete Greene, and come for them when they were wanted. They were long in arranging affairs satisfactorily, and were not a little startled at the close of their conference to find Frado missing. They thought approaching night would bring her. Twilight passed into darkness, and she did not come. They thought she had understood their plans, and had, perhaps, permanently withdrawn. They could not rest without making some effort to ascertain her retreat. Seth went in pursuit, and returned without her. They rallied others when they discovered that another little colored girl was missing, a favorite playmate of Frado's. All effort proved unavailing. Mag felt sure her fears were realized, and that she might never see her again. Before her anxieties became realities, both were safely returned, and from them and their attendant they learned that they went to walk, and not minding the direction soon found themselves lost. They had climbed fences and walls, passed through thickets and marshes, and when night approached selected a thick cluster of shrubbery as a covert for the night. They were discovered by the person who now restored them, chatting of their prospects, Frado attempting to banish the childish fears of her companion. As they were some miles from home, they were kindly cared for until morning. Mag was relieved to know her child was not driven to desperation by their intentions to relieve themselves of her, and she was inclined to think severe restraint would be healthful.

The removal was all arranged; the few days necessary for such migrations passed quickly, and one bright summer morning they bade farewell to their Singleton hovel, and with budgets and bundles commenced their weary march. As they neared the village, they heard the merry shouts of children gathered around the schoolroom, awaiting the coming of their teacher.

"Halloo!" screamed one, "Black, white and yeller!" "Black, white and yeller," echoed a dozen voices.

It did not grate so harshly on poor Mag as once it would. She did not even turn her head to look at them. She had passed into an insensibility no childish taunt could penetrate, else she would have reproached herself as she passed familiar scenes, for extending the separation once so easily annihilated by steadfast integrity. Two miles beyond lived the Bellmonts, in a large, old fashioned, two-story white house, environed by fruitful acres, and embellished by shrubbery and shade trees. Years ago a youthful couple consecrated it as home; and after many little feet had worn paths to favorite fruit trees, and over its green hills, and mingled at last with brother man in the race which belongs neither to the swift or strong, the sire became grey-haired and decrepid, and went to his last repose. His aged consort soon followed him. The old homestead thus passed into the hands of a son, to whose wife Mag had applied the epithet "she-devil," as may be remembered. John, the son,[7] had not in his family arrangements departed from the example of the father. The pastimes of his boyhood were ever freshly revived by witnessing the games of his own sons as they rallied about the same goal his youthful feet had often won; as well as by the amusements of his daughters in their imitations of maternal duties.

At the time we introduce them, however, John is wearing the badge of age. Most of his children were from home; some seeking employment; some were already settled in homes of their own. A maiden sister shared with him[8] the estate on which he resided, and occupied a portion of the house.

Within sight of the house, Seth seated himself with his bundles and the child he had been leading, while Mag walked onward to the house leading Frado. A knock at the door brought Mrs. Bellmont, and Mag asked if she would be willing to let that child stop there while she went to the Reed's house to wash, and when she came back she would call and get her. It seemed a novel request, but she consented. Why the impetuous child entered the house, we cannot tell; the door closed, and Mag hastily departed. Frado waited for the close of day, which was to bring back her mother. Alas! it never came. It was the last time she ever saw or heard of her mother.

CHAPTER III.

A NEW HOME FOR ME.[1]

Oh! did we but know of the shadows so nigh,
   The world would indeed be a prison of gloom;
All light would be quenched in youth's eloquent eye,
   And the prayer-lisping infant would ask for the tomb.

For if Hope be a star that may lead us astray,
   And "deceiveth the heart," as the aged ones preach;
Yet 'twas Mercy that gave it, to beacon our way,
   Though its halo illumes where it never can reach.

ELIZA COOK.[2]

As the day closed and Mag did not appear, surmises were expressed by the family that she never intended to return. Mr. Bellmont was a kind, humane man, who would not grudge hospitality to the poorest wanderer, nor fail to sympathize with any sufferer, however humble. The child's desertion by her mother appealed to his sympathy, and he felt inclined to succor her. To do this in opposition to Mrs. Bellmont's wishes, would be like encountering a whirlwind charged with fire, daggers and spikes. She was not as susceptible of fine emotions as her spouse. Mag's opinion of her was not without foundation. She was self-willed, haughty, undisciplined, arbitrary and severe. In common parlance, she was a *scold,* a thorough one. Mr. B.[3] remained silent during the consultation which follows, engaged in by mother, Mary[4] and John, or Jack,[5] as he was familiarly called.

"Send her to the County House," said Mary, in reply to the query what should be done with her, in a tone which indicated self-importance in the speaker. She was indeed the idol of her mother, and more nearly resembled her in disposition and manners than the others.

Jane, an invalid daughter, the eldest of those at home, was reclining on a sofa apparently uninterested.

"Keep her," said Jack. "She's real handsome and bright, and not very black, either."

"Yes," rejoined Mary; "that's just like you, Jack. She'll be of no use at all these three years, right under foot all the time."

"Poh! Miss Mary; if she should stay, it wouldn't be two days before you would be telling the girls about *our* nig, *our* nig!" retorted Jack.

"I don't want a nigger 'round *me,* do you, mother?" asked Mary.

"I don't mind the nigger in the child. I should like a dozen better than one," replied her mother. "If I could make her do my work in a few years,[6] I would keep her. I have so much trouble with girls I hire, I am almost persuaded if I have one to train up in my way from a child,[7] I shall be able to keep them awhile. I am tired of changing every few months."

"Where could she sleep?" asked Mary. "I don't want her near me."

"In the L chamber," answered the mother.

"How'll she get there?" asked Jack. "She'll be afraid to go through that dark passage, and she can't climb the ladder safely."

"She'll have to go there; it's good enough for a nigger," was the reply.

Jack was sent on horseback to ascertain if Mag was at her home. He returned with the testimony of Pete Greene that they were fairly departed, and that the child was intentionally thrust upon their family.

The imposition was not at all relished by Mrs. B., or the pert, haughty Mary, who had just glided into her teens.

"Show the child to bed, Jack," said his mother. "You seem most pleased with the little nigger, so you may introduce her to her room."

He went to the kitchen, and, taking Frado gently by the hand, told her he would put her in bed now; perhaps her mother would come the next night after her.

It was not yet quite dark, so they ascended the stairs without any light, passing through nicely furnished rooms, which were a source of great amazement to the child. He opened the door which connected with her room by a dark, unfinished passageway. "Don't bump your head," said Jack, and stepped before to open the door leading into her apartment,—an unfinished chamber over the kitchen, the roof slanting nearly to the floor, so that the bed could stand only in the middle of the room. A small half window furnished light and air. Jack returned to the sitting room with the remark that the child would soon outgrow those quarters.

"When she *does,* she'll outgrow the house," remarked the mother.

"What can she do to help you?" asked Mary. "She came just in the right time, didn't she? Just the very day after Bridget[8] left," continued she.

"I'll see what she can do in the morning," was the answer.

While this conversation was passing below, Frado lay, revolving in her little mind whether she would remain or not until her mother's return. She was of wilful, determined nature, a stranger to fear, and would not hesitate to wander away should she decide to. She remembered the conversation of her mother with Seth, the words "given away" which she heard used in reference to herself; and though she did not know their full import, she thought she should, by remaining, be in some relation to white people she was never favored with before. So she resolved to tarry, with the hope that mother would come and get her some time. The hot sun had penetrated her room, and it was long before a cooling breeze reduced the temperature so that she could sleep.

Frado was called early in the morning by her new mistress. Her first work was to feed the hens. She was shown how it was *always* to be done,[9] and in no other way; any departure from this rule to be punished by whipping. She was then accompanied by Jack to drive the cows to pasture, so she might learn the way. Upon her return she was allowed to eat her breakfast, consisting of a bowl of skimmed milk, with brown bread crusts, which she was told to eat, standing, by the kitchen table, and must not be over ten minutes about it. Meanwhile the family were taking their morning meal in the dining-room. This over, she was placed on a cricket to wash the common dishes; she was to be in waiting always to bring wood and chips, to run hither and thither from room to room.

A large amount of dish-washing for small hands followed dinner. Then the same after tea and going after the cows finished her first day's work. It was a new discipline to the child. She found some attractions about the place, and she retired to rest at night more willing to remain. The same routine followed day after day, with slight variation; adding a little more work, and spicing the toil with "words that burn," and frequent blows on her head. These were great annoyances to Frado, and had she known where her mother was, she would have gone at once to her. She was often greatly wearied, and silently wept over her sad fate. At first she wept aloud, which Mrs. Bellmont noticed by applying a raw-hide, always at hand in the kitchen. It was a symptom of discontent and complaining which must be "nipped in the bud," she said.

Thus passed a year. No intelligence of Mag. It was now certain Frado was to become a permanent member of the family. Her labors were multiplied; she was quite indispensable, although but seven years old. She had never learned to read, never heard of a school until her residence in the family.

Mrs. Bellmont was in doubt about the utility of attempting to educate people of color, who were incapable of elevation. This subject occasioned a lengthy discussion in the family. Mr. Bellmont, Jane and Jack arguing for Frado's education; Mary and her mother objecting. At last Mr. Bellmont declared decisively that she *should* go to school. He was a man who seldom decided controversies at home. The word once spoken admitted of no appeal; so, notwithstanding Mary's objection that she would have to attend the same school she did, the word became law.

It was to be a new scene to Frado, and Jack had many queries and conjectures to answer. He was himself too far advanced to attend the summer school, which Frado regretted, having had too many opportunities of witnessing Miss Mary's temper to feel safe in her company alone.

The opening day of school came. Frado sauntered on far in the rear of Mary, who was ashamed to be seen "walking with a nigger." As soon as she appeared, with scanty clothing and bared feet, the children assembled, noisily published her approach: "See that nigger,"[10] shouted one. "Look! look!" cried another. "I won't play with her," said one little girl. "Nor I neither," replied another.

Mary evidently relished these sharp attacks, and saw a fair prospect of lowering Nig where, according to her views, she belonged. Poor Frado, chagrined and grieved, felt that her anticipations of pleasure at such a place were far from being realized. She was just deciding to return home, and never come there again, when the teacher appeared, and observing the downcast looks of the child, took her by the hand, and led her into the school-room. All followed, and, after the bustle of securing seats was over, Miss Marsh[11] inquired if the children knew "any cause for the sorrow of that little girl?" pointing to Frado. It was soon all told. She then reminded them of their duties to the poor and friendless; their cowardice in attacking a young innocent child; referred them to one who looks not on outward appearances, but on the heart.[12] "She looks like a good girl; I think *I* shall love her, so lay aside all prejudice, and vie with each other in shewing kindness and good-will to one who seems different from you," were the closing remarks of the kind lady. Those kind words! The most agreeable sound which ever meets the ear of sorrowing, grieving childhood.

Example rendered her words efficacious. Day by day there was a manifest change of deportment towards "Nig." Her speeches often drew merriment from the children; no one could do more to enliven their favorite pastimes than Frado. Mary could not endure to see her thus noticed, yet knew not how to prevent it. She could not influence her schoolmates as she wished. She had not gained their affections by winning ways and yielding points of controversy. On the contrary, she was self-willed, domineering; every day reported "mad" by some of her companions. She availed herself of the only alternative, abuse and taunts, as they returned from school. This was not satisfactory; she wanted to use physical force "to subdue her," to "keep her down."

There was, on their way home, a field intersected by a stream over which a single plank was placed for a crossing. It occurred to Mary that it would be a punishment to Nig to compel her to cross over; so she dragged her to the edge, and told her authoritatively to go over. Nig hesitated, resisted. Mary placed herself behind the child, and, in the struggle to force her over, lost her footing and plunged into the stream. Some of the larger scholars being in sight, ran, and thus prevented Mary from drowning and Frado from falling. Nig scampered home fast as possible, and Mary went to the nearest house, dripping, to procure a change of garments. She came loitering home, half crying, exclaiming, "Nig pushed me into the stream!" She then related the particulars. Nig was called from the kitchen. Mary stood with anger flashing in her eyes. Mr. Bellmont sat quietly reading his paper. He had witnessed too many of Miss Mary's outbreaks to be startled. Mrs. Bellmont interrogated Nig.

"I didn't do it! I didn't do it!" answered Nig, passionately, and then related the occurrence truthfully.

The discrepancy greatly enraged Mrs. Bellmont. With loud accusations and angry gestures she approached the child. Turning to her husband, she asked,

"Will you sit still, there, and hear that black nigger call Mary a liar?"

"How do we know but she has told the truth? I shall not punish her," he replied, and left the house, as he usually did when a tempest threatened to envelop him. No sooner was he out of sight than Mrs. B. and Mary commenced beating her inhumanly; then propping her mouth open[13] with a piece of wood, shut her up in a dark room, without any supper. For employment, while the tempest raged within, Mr. Bellmont went for the cows, a task belonging to Frado, and thus unintentionally prolonged her pain. At dark Jack came in, and seeing Mary, accosted her with, "So you thought you'd vent your spite on Nig, did you? Why can't you let her alone? It was good enough for you to get a ducking, only you did not stay in half long enough."

"Stop!" said his mother. "You shall never talk so before me. You would have that little nigger trample on Mary, would you? She came home with a lie; it made Mary's story false."

"What was Mary's story?" asked Jack.

It was related.

"Now," said Jack, sallying into a chair, "the school-children happened to see it all, and they tell the same story Nig does.

Which is most likely to be true, what a dozen agree they saw, or the contrary?"

"It was very strange you will believe what others say against your sister," retorted his mother, with flashing eye. "I think it is time your father subdued you."

"Father is a sensible man," argued Jack. "He would not wrong a dog. Where *is* Frado?" he continued.

"Mother gave her a good whipping and shut her up," replied Mary.

Just then Mr. Bellmont entered, and asked if Frado was "shut up yet."

The knowledge of her innocence, the perfidy of his sister, worked fearfully on Jack. He bounded from his chair, searched every room till he found the child; her mouth wedged apart, her face swollen, and full of pain.

How Jack pitied her! He relieved her jaws, brought her some supper, took her to her room, comforted her as well as he knew how, sat by her till she fell asleep, and then left for the sitting room. As he passed his mother, he remarked, "If that was the way Frado was to be treated, he hoped she would never wake again!" He then imparted her situation to his father, who seemed untouched, till a glance at Jack exposed a tearful eye. Jack went early to her next morning. She awoke sad, but refreshed. After breakfast Jack took her with him to the field, and kept her through the day. But it could not be so generally. She must return to school, to her household duties. He resolved to do what he could to protect her from Mary and his mother. He bought her a dog, which became a great favorite with both. The invalid, Jane, would gladly befriend her; but she had not the strength to brave the iron will of her mother. Kind words and affectionate glances were the only expressions of sympathy she could safely indulge in. The men employed on the farm were always glad to hear her prattle; she was a great favorite with them. Mrs. Bellmont allowed them the privilege of talking with her in the kitchen. She did not fear but she should have ample opportunity of subduing her when they were away. Three months of schooling, summer and winter, she enjoyed for three years. Her winter over-dress was a cast-off overcoat, once worn by Jack, and a sun-bonnet. It was a source of great merriment to the scholars, but Nig's retorts were so mirthful, and their satisfaction so evident in attributing the selection to "Old Granny Bellmont," that it was not painful to Nig or pleasurable to Mary. Her jollity was not to be quenched by whipping or scolding. In Mrs. Bellmont's presence she was under restraint; but in the kitchen, and among her schoolmates, the pent up fires burst forth. She was ever at some sly prank when unseen by her teacher, in school hours; not unfrequently some outburst of merriment, of which she was the original, was charged upon some innocent mate, and punishment inflicted which she merited. They enjoyed her antics so fully that any of them would suffer wrongfully to keep open the avenues of mirth. She would venture far beyond propriety, thus shielded and countenanced.

The teacher's desk was supplied with drawers, in which were stored his books and other *et ceteras* of the profession. The children observed Nig very busy there one morning before school, as they flitted in occasionally from their play outside. The master came; called the children to order; opened a drawer to take the book the occasion required; when out poured a volume of smoke. "Fire! fire!" screamed he, at the top of his voice. By the time he had become sufficiently acquainted with the peculiar odor, to know he was imposed upon. The scholars shouted with laughter to see the terror of the dupe, who, feeling abashed at the needless fright, made no very strict investigation, and Nig once more escaped punishment. She had provided herself with cigars, and puffing, puffing away at the crack of the drawer, had filled it with smoke, and then closed it tightly to deceive the teacher, and amuse the scholars. The interim of terms was filled up with a variety of duties new and peculiar. At home, no matter how powerful the heat when sent to rake hay or guard the grazing herd, she was never permitted to shield her skin from the sun.[14] She was not many shades darker than Mary now; what a calamity it would be ever to hear the contrast spoken of.[15] Mrs. Bellmont was determined the sun should have full power to darken the shade which nature had first bestowed upon her as best befitting.

CHAPTER IV.

A FRIEND FOR NIG.

"Hours of my youth! when nurtured in my breast,
To love a stranger, friendship made me blest;—
Friendship, the dear peculiar bond of youth,
When every artless bosom throbs with truth;
Untaught by worldly wisdom how to feign;
And check each impulse with prudential reign;
When all we feel our honest souls disclose—
In love to friends, in open hate to foes;
No varnished tales the lips of youth repeat,
No dear-bought knowledge purchased by deceit."

BYRON.[1]

With what differing emotions have the denizens of earth awaited the approach of to-day. Some sufferer has counted the vibrations of the pendulum impatient for its dawn, who, now that it has arrived, is anxious for its close. The votary of pleasure, conscious of yesterday's void, wishes for power to arrest time's haste till a few more hours of mirth shall be enjoyed. The unfortunate are yet grazing in vain for golden-edged clouds they fancied would appear in their horizon. The good man feels that he has accomplished too little for the Master, and sighs that another day must so soon close. Innocent childhood, weary of its stay, longs for another morrow; busy manhood cries, hold! hold! and pursues it to another's dawn. All are dissatisfied. All crave some good not yet possessed, which time is expected to bring with all its morrows.

Was it strange that, to a disconsolate child, three years should seem a long, long time? During school time she had rest from Mrs. Bellmont's tyranny. She was now nine years old; time, her mistress said, such privileges should cease.

She could now read and spell, and knew the elementary steps

in grammar, arithmetic, and writing. Her education completed, as *she* said, Mrs. Bellmont felt that her time and person belonged solely to her. She was under her in every sense of the word. What an opportunity to indulge her vixen nature! No matter what occurred to ruffle her, or from what source provocation came, real or fancied, a few blows on Nig seemed to relieve her of a portion of ill-will.

These were days when Fido was the entire confidant of Frado. She told him her griefs as though he were human; and he sat so still, and listened so attentively, she really believed he knew her sorrows. All the leisure moments she could gain were used in teaching him some feat of dog-agility, so that Jack pronounced him very knowing, and was truly gratified to know he had furnished her with a gift answering his intentions.

Fido was the constant attendant of Frado, when sent from the house on errands, going and returning with the cows, out in the fields, to the village. If ever she forgot her hardships it was in his company.

Spring was now retiring. James,[2] one of the absent sons, was expected home on a visit. He had never seen the last acquisition to the family. Jack had written faithfully of all the merits of his colored *protegé,* and hinted plainly that mother did not always treat her just right. Many were the preparations to make the visit pleasant, and as the day approached when he was to arrive, great exertions were made to cook the favorite viands, to prepare the choicest table-fare.

The morning of the arrival day was a busy one. Frado knew not who would be of so much importance; her feet were speeding hither and thither so unsparingly. Mrs. Bellmont seemed a trifle fatigued, and her shoes which had, early in the morning, a methodic squeak, altered to an irregular, peevish snap.

"Get some little wood to make the fire burn," said Mrs. Bellmont, in a sharp tone. Frado obeyed, bringing the smallest she could find.

Mrs. Bellmont approached her, and, giving her a box on her ear, reiterated the command.

The first the child brought was the smallest to be found; of course, the second must be a trifle larger. She well knew it was, as she threw it into a box on the hearth. To Mrs. Bellmont it was a greater affront, as well as larger wood, so she "taught her" with the raw-hide, and sent her the third time for "little wood."

Nig, weeping, knew not what to do. She had carried the smallest; none left would suit her mistress; of course further punishment awaited her; so she gathered up whatever came first, and threw it down on the hearth. As she expected, Mrs. Bellmont, enraged, approached her, and kicked her so forcibly as to throw her upon the floor. Before she could rise, another foiled the attempt, and then followed kick after kick in quick succession and power, till she reached the door. Mr. Bellmont and Aunt Abby, hearing the noise, rushed in, just in time to see the last of the performance. Nig jumped up, and rushed from the house, out of sight.

Aunt Abby returned to her apartment, followed by John, who was muttering to himself.

"What were you saying?" asked Aunt Abby.

"I said I hoped the child never would come into the house again."

"What would become of her? You cannot mean *that,*" continued his sister.

"I do mean it. The child does as much work as a woman ought to; and just see how she is kicked about!"

"Why do you have it so, John?" asked his sister.

"How am I to help it? Women rule the earth, and all in it."

"I think I should rule my own house, John,"—

"And live in hell meantime," added Mr. Bellmont.

John now sauntered out to the barn to await the quieting of the storm.

Aunt Abby[3] had a glimpse of Nig as she passed out of the yard; but to arrest her, or shew her that *she* would shelter her, in Mrs. Bellmont's presence, would only bring reserved wrath on her defenceless head. Her sister-in-law had great prejudices against her. One cause of the alienation was that she did not give her right in the homestead to John, and leave it forever; another was that she was a professor of religion, (so was Mrs. Bellmont;) but Nab, as she called her, did not live according to her profession; another, that she *would* sometimes give Nig cake and pie, which she was never allowed to have at home. Mary had often noticed and spoken of her inconsistencies.

The dinner hour passed. Frado had not appeared. Mrs. B. made no inquiry or search. Aunt Abby looked long, and found her concealed in an outbuilding. "Come into the house with me," implored Aunt Abby.

"I ain't going in any more," sobbed the child.

"What will you do?" asked Aunt Abby.

"I've got to stay out here and die. I ha'n't got no mother, no home. I wish I was dead."

"Poor thing," muttered Aunt Abby; and slyly providing her with some dinner, left her to her grief.

Jane[4] went to confer with her Aunt about the affair; and learned from her the retreat. She would gladly have concealed her in her own chamber, and ministered to her wants; but she was dependent on Mary and her mother for care, and any displeasure caused by attention to Nig, was seriously felt.

Toward night the coach brought James. A time of general greeting, inquiries for absent members of the family, a visit to Aunt Abby's room, undoing a few delicacies for Jane, brought them to the tea hour.

"Where's Frado?" asked Mr. Bellmont, observing she was not in her usual place, behind her mistress' chair.

"I don't know, and I don't care. If she makes her appearance again, I'll take the skin from her body," replied his wife.

James, a fine looking young man, with a pleasant countenance, placid, and yet decidedly serious, yet not stern, looked up confounded. He was no stranger to his mother's nature; but years of absence had erased the occurrences once so familiar, and he asked, "Is this that pretty little Nig, Jack writes to me about, that you are so severe upon, mother?"

"I'll not leave much of her beauty to be seen, if she comes in sight; and now, John," said Mrs. B., turning to her husband, "you need not think you are going to learn her to treat me in this way; just see how saucy she was this morning. She shall learn her place."

Mr. Bellmont raised his calm, determined eye full upon her,

and said, in a decisive manner: "You shall not strike, or scald, or skin her, as you call it, if she comes back again. Remember!" and he brought his hand down upon the table. "I have searched an hour for her now, and she is not to be found on the premises. Do *you* know where she is? Is she *your* prisoner?"

"No! I have just told you I did not know where she was. Nab had her hid somewhere, I suppose. Oh, dear! I did not think it would come to this; that my own husband would treat me so." Then came fast flowing tears, which no one but Mary seemed to notice. Jane crept into Aunt Abby's room; Mr. Bellmont and James went out of doors, and Mary remained to condole with her parent.

"Do you know where Frado is?" asked Jane of her aunt.

"No," she replied. "I have hunted everywhere. She has left her first hiding-place. I cannot think what has become of her. There comes Jack and Fido; perhaps he knows;" and she walked to a window near, where James and his father were conversing together.

The two brothers exchanged a hearty greeting, and then Mr. Bellmont told Jack to eat his supper; afterward he wished to send him away. He immediately went in. Accustomed to all the phases of indoor storms, from a whine to thunder and lightning, he saw at a glance marks of disturbance. He had been absent through the day with the hired men.

"What's the fuss?" asked he, rushing into Aunt Abby's.

"Eat your supper," said Jane, "go home, Jack."

Back again through the dining-room, and out to his father.

"What's the fuss?" again inquired he of his father.

"Eat your supper, Jack, and see if you can find Frado. She's not been seen since morning, and then she was kicked out of the house."

"I shan't eat my supper till I find her," said Jack, indignantly. "Come, James, and see the little creature mother treats so."

They started, calling, searching, coaxing, all their way along. No Frado. They returned to the house to consult. James and Jack declared they would not sleep till she was found.

Mrs. Bellmont attempted to dissuade them from the search. "It was a shame a little *nigger* should make so much trouble."

Just then Fido came running up, and Jack exclaimed, "Fido knows where she is, I'll bet."

"So I believe," said his father; "but we shall not be wiser unless we can outwit him. He will not do what his mistress forbids him."

"I know how to fix him," said Jack. Taking a plate from the table, which was still waiting, he called, "Fido! Fido! Frado wants some supper. Come!" Jack started, the dog followed, and soon capered on before, far, far into the fields, over walls and through fences, into a piece of swampy land. Jack followed close, and soon appeared to James, who was quite in the rear, coaxing and forcing Frado along with him.

A frail child, driven from shelter by the cruelty of his mother, was an object of interest to James. They persuaded her to go home with them, warmed her by the kitchen fire, gave her a good supper, and took her with them into the sitting-room.

"Take that nigger out of my sight," was Mrs. Bellmont's command, before they could be seated.

James led her into Aunt Abby's, where he knew they were welcome. They chatted awhile until Frado seemed cheerful; then James led her to her room, and waited until she retired.

"Are you glad I've come home?" asked James.

"Yes; if you won't let me be whipped tomorrow."

"You won't be whipped. You must try to be a good girl," counselled James.

"If I do, I get whipped;" sobbed the child. "They won't believe what I say. Oh, I wish I had my mother back; then I should not be kicked and whipped so. Who made me so?"

"God;" answered James.

"Did God make you?"

"Yes."

"Who made Aunt Abby?"

"God."

"Who made your mother?"

"God."

"Did the same God that made her make me?"

"Yes."

"Well, then, I don't like him."

"Why not?"

"Because he made her white, and me black. Why didn't he make us *both* white?"

"I don't know; try to go to sleep, and you will feel better in the morning," was all the reply he could make to her knotty queries. It was a long time before she fell asleep; and a number of days before James felt in a mood to visit and entertain old associates and friends.

CHAPTER V.

DEPARTURES.

Life is a strange avenue of various trees and flowers;
Lightsome at commencement, but darkening to its end in a distant, massy portal.
It beginneth as a little path, edged with the violet and primrose,
A little path of lawny grass and soft to tiny feet.
Soon, spring thistles in the way.

TUPPER.[1]

James's visit concluded. Frado had become greatly attached to him, and with sorrow she listened and joined in the farewells which preceded his exit. The remembrance of his kindness cheered her through many a weary month, and an occasional word to her in letters to Jack, were like "cold waters to a thirsty soul."[2] Intelligence came that James would soon marry; Frado hoped he would, and remove her from such severe treatment as she was subject to. There had been additional burdens laid on her since his return. She must now *milk* the cows, she had then only to drive. Flocks of sheep had been added to the farm, which daily claimed a portion of her time. In the absence of the men, she must harness the horse for Mary and her mother to ride, go to mill, in short, do the work of a boy, could one be procured to endure the tirades of Mrs. Bellmont. She was first up in the morning, doing what she could towards breakfast. Occasionally, she would utter some funny thing for Jack's benefit, while she was waiting on the table, provoking a sharp look from his mother, or expulsion from the room.

On one such occasion, they found her on the roof of the barn. Some repairs having been necessary, a staging had been erected, and was not wholly removed. Availing herself of ladders, she was mounted in high glee on the topmost board. Mr. Bellmont called sternly for her to come down; poor Jane nearly fainted from fear.

Mrs. B. and Mary did not care if she "broke her neck," while Jack and the men laughed at her fearlessness. Strange, one spark of playfulness could remain amid such constant toil; but her natural temperament was in a high degree mirthful, and the encouragement she received from Jack and the hired men, constantly nurtured the inclination. When she had none of the family around to be merry with, she would amuse herself with the animals. Among the sheep was a willful leader, who always persisted in being first served, and many times in his fury he had thrown down Nig, till, provoked, she resolved to punish him. The pasture in which the sheep grazed was bounded on three sides by a wide stream, which flowed on one side at the base of precipitous banks. The first spare moments at her command, she ran to the pasture with a dish in her hand, and mounting the highest point of land nearest the stream, called the flock to their mock repast. Mr. Bellmont, with his laborers, were in sight, though unseen by Frado. They paused to see what she was about to do. Should she by any mishap lose her footing, she must roll into the stream, and, without aid, must drown. They thought of shouting; but they feared an unexpected salute might startle her, and thus ensure what they were anxious to prevent. They watched in breathless silence. The willful sheep came furiously leaping and bounding far in advance of the flock. Just as he leaped for the dish, she suddenly jumped one side, when down he rolled into the river, and swimming across, remained alone till night. The men lay down, convulsed with laughter at the trick, and guessed at once its object. Mr. Bellmont talked seriously to the child for exposing herself to such danger; but she hopped about on her toes, and with laughable grimaces replied, she knew she was quick enough to "give him a slide."

But to return. James married a Baltimorean lady of wealthy parentage, an indispensable requisite, his mother had always taught him. He did not marry her wealth, though; he loved *her,* sincerely. She was not unlike his sister Jane, who had a social, gentle, loving nature, rather *too* yielding, her brother thought. His Susan[3] had a firmness which Jane needed to complete her character, but which her ill health may in a measure have failed to produce. Although an invalid, she was not excluded from society. Was it strange *she* should seem a desirable companion, a treasure as a wife?

Two young men seemed desirous of possessing her. One was a neighbor, Henry Reed,[4] a tall, spare young man, with sandy hair, and blue, sinister eyes. He seemed to appreciate her wants, and watch with interest her improvement or decay. His kindness she received, and by it was almost won. Her mother wished her to encourage his attentions. She had counted the acres which were to be transmitted to an only son; she knew there was silver in the purse; she would not have Jane too sentimental.

The eagerness with which he amassed wealth, was repulsive to Jane; he did not spare his person or beasts in its pursuit. She felt that to such a man she should be considered an incumbrance; she doubted if he would desire her, if he did not know she would bring a handsome patrimony. Her mother, full in favor with the parents of Henry, commanded her to accept him. She engaged herself, yielding to her mother's wishes, because she had not strength to oppose them; and sometimes, when witness of her mother's and Mary's tyranny, she felt any change would be preferable, even such a one as this. She knew her husband should be the man of her own selecting, one she was conscious of preferring before all others. She could not say this of Henry.

In this dilemma, a visitor came to Aunt Abby's; one of her boy-favorites, George Means,[5] from an adjoining State. Sensible, plain looking, agreeable, talented, he could not long be a stranger to any one who wished to know him. Jane was accustomed to sit much with Aunt Abby always; her presence now seemed necessary to assist in entertaining this youthful friend. Jane was more pleased with him each day, and silently wished Henry possessed more refinement, and the polished manners of George. She felt dissatisfied with her relation to him. His calls while George was there, brought their opposing qualities vividly before her, and she found it disagreeable to force herself into those attentions belonging to him. She received him apparently only as a neighbor.

George returned home, and Jane endeavored to stifle the risings of dissatisfaction, and had nearly succeeded, when a letter came which needed but one glance to assure her of its birthplace; and she retired for its perusal. Well was it for her that her mother's suspicion was not aroused, or her curiosity startled to inquire who it came from. After reading it, she glided into Aunt Abby's, and placed it in her hands, who was no stranger to Jane's trials.

George could not rest after his return, he wrote, until he had communicated to Jane the emotions her presence awakened, and his desire to love and possess her as his own. He begged to know if his affections were reciprocated, or could be; if she would permit him to write to her; if she was free from all obligation to another.

"What would mother say?" queried Jane, as she received the letter from her aunt.

"Not much to comfort you."

"Now, aunt, George is just such a man as I could really love, I think, from all I have seen of him; you know I never could say that of Henry"—

"Then don't marry him," interrupted Aunt Abby.

"Mother will make me."

"Your father won't."

"Well, aunt, what can I do? Would you answer the letter, or not?"

"Yes, answer it. Tell him your situation."

"I shall not tell him all my feelings."

Jane answered that she had enjoyed his company much; she had seen nothing offensive in his manner or appearance; that she was under no obligations which forbade her receiving letters from him as a friend and acquaintance. George was puzzled by the reply. He wrote to Aunt Abby, and from her learned all. He could not see Jane thus sacrificed, without making an effort to rescue her. Another visit followed. George heard Jane say she preferred *him*. He then conferred with Henry at his home. It was not a pleasant subject to talk upon. To be thus supplanted, was not to be thought of. He would sacrifice everything but his inheritance to secure his betrothed.

"And so you are the cause of her late coldness towards me. Leave! I will talk no more about it; the business is settled between us; there it will remain," said Henry.

"Have you no wish to know the real state of Jane's affections towards you?" asked George.

"No! Go, I say! go!" and Henry opened the door for him to pass out.

He retired to Aunt Abby's. Henry soon followed, and presented his cause to Mrs. Bellmont.

Provoked, surprised, indignant, she summoned Jane to her presence, and after a lengthy tirade upon Nab, and her satanic influence, told her she could not break the bonds which held her to Henry; she should not. George Means was rightly named; he was, truly, mean enough; she knew his family of old; his father had four wives, and five times as many children.

"Go to your room, Miss Jane," she continued. "Don't let me know of your being in Nab's for one while."

The storm was now visible to all beholders. Mr. Bellmont sought Jane. She told him her objections to Henry; showed him George's letter; told her answer, the occasion of his visit. He bade her not make herself sick; he would see that she was not compelled to violate her free choice in so important a transaction. He then sought the two young men; told them he could not as a father see his child compelled to an uncongenial union; a free, voluntary choice was of such importance to one of her health. She must be left free to her own choice.

Jane sent Henry a letter of dismission; he sent her one of a legal bearing, in which he balanced his disappointment by a few hundreds.

To brave her mother's fury, nearly overcame her, but the consolations of a kind father and aunt cheered her on. After a suitable interval she was married to George, and removed to his home in Vermont. Thus another light disappeared from Nig's horizon. Another was soon to follow. Jack was anxious to try his skill in providing for his own support; so a situation as clerk in a store was procured in a Western city,[6] and six months after Jane's departure, was Nig abandoned to the tender mercies of Mary and her mother. As if to remove the last vestige of earthly joy, Mrs. Bellmont sold the companion and pet of Frado, the dog Fido.

CHAPTER VI.

VARIETIES.

> "Hard are life's early steps; and but that youth is buoyant, confident, and strong in hope, men would behold its threshold and despair."[1]

The sorrow of Frado was very great for her pet, and Mr. Bellmont by great exertion obtained it again, much to the relief of the child. To be thus deprived of all her sources of pleasure was a sure way to exalt their worth, and Fido became, in her estimation, a more valuable presence than the human beings who surrounded her.

James had now been married a number of years, and frequent requests for a visit from the family were at last accepted, and Mrs. Bellmont made great preparations for a fall sojourn in Baltimore. Mary was installed housekeeper—in name merely, for Nig was the only moving power in the house. Although suffering from their joint severity, she felt safer than to be thrown wholly upon an ardent, passionate, unrestrained young lady, whom she always hated and felt it hard to be obliged to obey. The trial she must meet. Were Jack or Jane at home she would have some refuge; one only remained; good Aunt Abby was still in the house.

She saw the fast receding coach which conveyed her master and mistress with regret, and begged for one favor only, that James would send for her when they returned, a hope she had confidently cherished all these five years.

She was now able to do all the washing, ironing, baking, and the common *et cetera* of the household duties, though but fourteen. Mary left all for her to do, though she affected great responsibility. She would show herself in the kitchen long enough to relieve herself of some command, better withheld; or insist upon some compliance to her wishes in some department which she was very imperfectly acquainted with, very much less than the person she was addressing; and so impetuous till her orders were obeyed, that to escape the turmoil, Nig would often go contrary to her own knowledge to gain a respite.

Nig was taken sick! What could be done? The *work*, certainly, but not by Miss Mary. So Nig would work while she could remain erect, then sink down upon the floor, or a chair, till she could rally for a fresh effort. Mary would look in upon her, chide her for her laziness, threaten to tell mother when she came home, and so forth.

"Nig!" screamed Mary, one of her sickest days, "come here, and sweep these threads from the carpet." She attempted to drag her weary limbs along, using the broom as support. Impatient of delay, she called again, but with a different request. "Bring me some wood, you lazy jade, quick." Nig rested the broom against the wall and started on the fresh behest.

Too long gone. Flushed with anger, she rose and greeted her with, "What are you gone so long, for? Bring it in quick, I say."

"I am coming as quick as I can," she replied, entering the door.

"Saucy, impudent nigger, you! is the way you answer me?" and taking a large carving knife from the table, she hurled it, in her rage, at the defenceless girl.

Dodging quickly, it fastened in the ceiling a few inches from where she stood. There rushed on Mary's mental vision a picture of bloodshed, in which she was the perpetrator, and the sad consequences of what was so nearly an actual occurrence.

"Tell anybody of this, if you dare. If you tell Aunt Abby, I'll certainly kill you," said she, terrified. She returned to her room, brushed her threads herself; was for a day or two more guarded, and so escaped deserved and merited penalty.

Oh, how long the weeks seemed which held Nig in subjection to Mary; but they passed like all earth's sorrows and joys. Mr. and Mrs. B. returned delighted with their visit, and laden with rich presents for Mary. No word of hope for Nig. James was quite unwell, and would come home the next spring for a visit.

This, thought Nig, will be my time of release. I shall go back with him.

From early dawn until after all were retired,[2] was she toiling, overworked, disheartened, longing for relief.

Exposure from heat to cold, or the reverse, often destroyed her health for short intervals. She wore no shoes[3] until after frost, and snow even, appeared; and bared her feet again before the last vestige of winter disappeared. These sudden changes she was so illy guarded against, nearly conquered her physical system. Any word of complaint was severely repulsed or cruelly punished.

She was told she had much more than she deserved. So that manual labor was not in reality her only burden; but such an incessant torrent of scolding and boxing and threatening, was enough to deter one of maturer years from remaining within sound of the strife.

It is impossible to give an impression of the manifest enjoyment of Mrs. B. in these kitchen scenes. It was her favorite exercise to enter the apartment noisily, vociferate orders, give a few sudden blows to quicken Nig's pace, then return to the sitting room with *such* a satisfied expression, congratulating herself upon her thorough house-keeping qualities.

She usually rose in the morning at the ringing of the bell for breakfast; if she were heard stirring before that time, Nig knew well there was an extra amount of scolding to be borne.

No one now stood between herself and Frado, but Aunt Abby. And if *she* dared to interfere in the least, she was ordered back to her "own quarters." Nig would creep slyly into her room, learn what she could of her regarding the absent, and thus gain some light in the thick gloom of care and toil and sorrow in which she was immersed.

The first of spring a letter came from James, announcing declining health. He must try northern air as a restorative; so Frado joyfully prepared for this agreeable increase of the family, this addition to her cares.

He arrived feeble, lame, from his disease, so changed Frado wept at his appearance, fearing he would be removed from her forever. He kindly greeted her, took her to the parlor to see his wife and child, and said many things to kindle smiles on her sad face.

Frado felt so happy in his presence, so safe from maltreatment! He was to her a shelter. He observed, silently, the ways of the house a few days; Nig still took her meals in the same manner as formerly, having the same allowance of food. He, one day, bade her not remove the food, but sit down to the table and eat.

"She *will,* mother," said he, calmly, but imperatively; "I'm determined; she works hard; I've watched her. Now, while I stay, she is going to sit down *here,* and eat such food as we eat."

A few sparks from the mother's black eyes were the only reply; she feared to oppose where she knew she could not prevail. So Nig's standing attitude, and selected diet vanished.

Her clothing was yet poor and scanty; she was not blessed with a Sunday attire; for she was never permitted to attend church with her mistress. "Religion was not meant for niggers," *she* said; when the husband and brothers were absent, she would drive Mrs. B. and Mary there, then return, and go for them at the close of the service, but never remain. Aunt Abby would take her to evening meetings, held in the neighborhood, which Mrs. B. never attended; and impart to her lessons of truth and grace as they walked to the place of prayer.

Many of less piety would scorn to present so doleful a figure; Mrs. B. had shaved her glossy ringlets; and, in her coarse cloth gown and ancient bonnet, she was anything but an enticing object.[4] But Aunt Abby looked within. She saw a soul to save, an immortality of happiness to secure.

These evenings were eagerly anticipated by Nig; it was such a pleasant release from labor.

Such perfect contrast in the melody and prayers of these good people to the harsh tones which fell on her ears during the day.

Soon she had all their sacred songs at command, and enlivened her toil by accompanying it with this melody.

James encouraged his aunt in her efforts. He had found the *Saviour,* he wished to have Frado's desolate heart gladdened, quieted, sustained, by *His* presence. He felt sure there were elements in her heart which, transformed and purified by the gospel, would make her worthy the esteem and friendship of the world. A kind, affectionate heart, native wit, and common sense, and the pertness she sometimes exhibited, he felt if restrained properly, might become useful in originating a self-reliance which would be of service to her in after years.

Yet it was not possible to compass all this, while she remained where she was. He wished to be cautious about pressing too closely her chains on his mother, as it would increase the burdened one he so anxiously wished to relieve. He cheered her on with the hope of returning with his family, when he recovered sufficiently.

Nig seemed awakened to new hopes and aspirations, and realized a longing for the future, hitherto unknown.

To complete Nig's enjoyment, Jack arrived unexpectedly. His greeting was as hearty to herself as to any of the family.

"Where are your curls, Fra?" asked Jack, after the usual salutation.

"Your mother cut them off."

"Thought you were getting handsome, did she? Same old story, is it; knocks and bumps? Better times coming; never fear, Nig."

How different this appellative sounded from him; he said it in such a tone, with such a rogueish look!

She laughed, and replied that he had better take her West for a housekeeper.

Jack was pleased with James's innovations of table discipline, and would often tarry in the dining-room, to see Nig in her new place at the family table. As he was thus sitting one day, after the family had finished dinner, Frado seated herself in her mistress' chair, and was just reaching for a clean dessert plate which was on the table, when her mistress entered.

"Put that plate down; you shall not have a clean one; eat from mine," continued she. Nig hesitated. To eat after James, his wife or Jack, would have been pleasant; but to be commanded to do what was disagreeable by her mistress, *because* it was disagreeable, was trying. Quickly looking about, she took the plate, called Fido to wash it, which he did to the best of his ability; then, wiping her knife and fork on the cloth, she proceeded to eat her dinner.

Nig never looked toward her mistress during the process. She had Jack near; she did not fear her now.

Insulted, full of rage, Mrs. Bellmont rushed to her husband,

and commanded him to notice this insult; to whip that child; if he would not do it, James ought.

James came to hear the kitchen version of the affair. Jack was boiling over with laughter. He related all the circumstances to James, and pulling a bright, silver half-dollar from his pocket, he threw it at Nig, saying, "There, take that; 't was worth paying for."

James sought his mother; told her he "would not excuse or palliate Nig's impudence; but she should not be whipped or be punished at all. You have not treated her, mother, so as to gain her love; she is only exhibiting your remissness in this matter."

She only smothered her resentment until a convenient opportunity offered. The first time she was left alone with Nig, she gave her a thorough beating, to bring up arrearages; and threatened, if she ever exposed her to James, she would "cut her tongue out."

James found her, upon his return, sobbing; but fearful of revenge, she dared not answer his queries. He guessed their cause, and longed for returning health to take her under his protection.

CHAPTER VII.
SPIRITUAL CONDITION OF NIG.

"What are our joys but dreams? and what our hopes
But goodly shadows in the summer cloud?"

H. K. W.[1]

James did not improve as was hoped. Month after month passed away, and brought no prospect of returning health. He could not walk far from the house for want of strength; but he loved to sit with Aunt Abby in her quiet room, talking of unseen glories, and heart-experiences, while planning for the spiritual benefit of those around them. In these confidential interviews, Frado was never omitted. They would discuss the prevalent opinion of the public, that people of color are really inferior; incapable of cultivation and refinement. They would glance at the qualities of Nig, which promised so much if rightly directed. "I wish you would take her, James, when you are well, home with *you,*" said Aunt Abby, in one of these seasons.

"Just what I am longing to do, Aunt Abby. Susan is just of my mind, and we intend to take her; I have been wishing to do so for years."

"She seems much affected by what she hears at the evening meetings, and asks me many questions on serious things; seems to love to read the Bible; I feel hopes of her."

"I hope she *is* thoughtful; no one has a kinder heart, one capable of loving more devotedly. But to think how prejudiced the world are towards her people; that she must be reared in such ignorance as to drown all the finer feelings. When I think of what she might be, of what she will be, I feel like grasping time till opinions change, and thousands like her rise into a noble freedom. I have seen Frado's grief, because she is black, amount to agony. It makes me sick to recall these scenes. Mother pretends to think she don't know enough to sorrow for anything; but if she could see her as I have, when she supposed herself entirely alone, except her little dog Fido, lamenting her loneliness and complexion, I think, if she is not past feeling, she would retract. In the summer I was walking near the barn, and as I stood I heard sobs. 'Oh! oh!' I heard, 'why was I made? why can't I die? Oh, what have I to live for? No one cares for me only to get my work. And I feel sick; who cares for that? Work as long as I can stand, and then fall down and lay there till I can get up. No mother, father, brother or sister to care for me, and then it is, You lazy nigger, lazy nigger—all because I am black! Oh, if I could die!'

"I stepped into the barn, where I could see her. She was crouched down by the hay with her faithful friend Fido, and as she ceased speaking, buried her face in her hands, and cried bitterly; then, patting Fido, she kissed him, saying, 'You love me, Fido, don't you? but we must go work in the field.' She started on her mission; I called her to me, and told her she need not go, the hay was doing well.

"She has such confidence in me that she will do just as I tell her; so we found a seat under a shady tree, and there I took the opportunity to combat the notions she seemed to entertain respecting the loneliness of her condition and want of sympathizing friends. I assured her that mother's views were by no means general; that in our part of the country there were thousands upon thousands who favored the elevation of her race, disapproving of oppression in all its forms; that she was not unpitied, friendless, and utterly despised; that she might hope for better things in the future. Having spoken these words of comfort, I rose with the resolution that if I recovered my health I would take her home with me, whether mother was willing or not."

"I don't know what your mother would do without her; still, I wish she was away."

Susan now came for her long absent husband, and they returned home to their room.

The month of November was one of great anxiety on James's account. He was rapidly wasting away.

A celebrated physician was called, and performed a surgical operation, as a last means. Should this fail, there was no hope. Of course he was confined wholly to his room, mostly to his bed. With all his bodily suffering, all his anxiety for his family, whom he might not live to protect, he did not forget Frado. He shielded her from many beatings, and every day imparted religious instructions. No one, but his wife, could move him so easily as Frado; so that in addition to her daily toil she was often deprived of her rest at night.

Yet she insisted on being called; she wished to show her love for one who had been such a friend to her. Her anxiety and grief increased as the probabilities of his recovery became doubtful.

Mrs. Bellmont found her weeping on his account, shut her up, and whipped her with the raw-hide, adding an injunction never to be seen snivelling again because she had a little work to do. She was very careful never to shed tears on his account, in her presence, afterwards.

CHAPTER VIII.

VISITOR AND DEPARTURE.

—"Other cares engross me, and my tired soul with emulative haste,
Looks to its God."[1]

The brother associated with James in business, in Baltimore, was sent for to confer with one who might never be able to see him there.

James began to speak of life as closing; of heaven, as of a place in immediate prospect; of aspirations, which waited for fruition in glory. His brother, Lewis[2] by name, was an especial favorite of sister Mary; more like her, in disposition and preferences than James or Jack.

He arrived as soon as possible after the request, and saw with regret the sure indications of fatality in his sick brother, and listened to his admonitions—admonitions to a Christian life—with tears, and uttered some promises of attention to the subject so dear to the heart of James.

How gladly he would have extended healing aid. But, alas! it was not in his power; so, after listening to his wishes and arrangements for his family and business, he decided to return home.

Anxious for company home, he persuaded his father and mother to permit Mary to attend him. She was not at all needed in the sick room; she did not choose to be useful in the kitchen, and then she was fully determined to go.

So all the trunks were assembled and crammed with the best selections from the wardrobe of herself and mother, where the last-mentioned articles could be appropriated.

"Nig was never so helpful before," Mary remarked, and wondered what had induced such a change in place of former sullenness.

Nig was looking further than the present, and congratulating herself upon some days of peace, for Mary never lost opportunity of informing her mother of Nig's delinquincies, were she otherwise ignorant.

Was it strange if she were officious, with such relief in prospect?

The parting from the sick brother was tearful and sad. James prayed in their presence for their renewal in holiness; and urged their immediate attention to eternal realities, and gained a promise that Susan and Charlie[3] should share their kindest regards.

No sooner were they on their way, than Nig slyly crept round to Aunt Abby's room, and tiptoeing and twisting herself into all shapes, she exclaimed,—

"She's gone, Aunt Abby, she's gone, fairly gone"; and jumped up and down, till Aunt Abby feared she would attract the noise of her mistress by such demonstrations.

"Well, she's gone, gone, Aunt Abby. I hope she'll never come back again."

"No! no! Frado, that's wrong! you would be wishing her dead; that won't do."

"Well, I'll bet she'll never come back again; somehow, I feel as though she wouldn't."

"She is James's sister," remonstrated Aunt Abby.

"So is our cross sheep just as much, that I ducked in the river; I'd like to try my hand at curing *her* too."

"But you forget what our good minister told us last week, about doing good to those that hate us."

"Didn't I do good, Aunt Abby, when I washed and ironed and packed her old duds to get rid of her, and helped her pack her trunks, and run here and there for her?"

"Well, well, Frado; you must go finish your work, or your mistress will be after you, and remind you severely of Miss Mary, and some others beside."

Nig went as she was told, and her clear voice was heard as she went, singing in joyous notes the relief she felt at the removal of one of her tormentors.

Day by day the quiet of the sick man's room was increased. He was helpless and nervous; and often wished change of position, thereby hoping to gain momentary relief. The calls upon Frado were consequently more frequent, her nights less tranquil. Her health was impaired by lifting the sick man, and by drudgery in the kitchen. Her ill health she endeavored to conceal from James, fearing he might have less repose if there should be a change of attendants; and Mrs. Bellmont, she well knew, would have no sympathy for her. She was at last so much reduced as to be unable to stand erect for any great length of time. She would *sit* at the table to wash her dishes; if she heard the well-known step of her mistress, she would rise till she returned to her room, and then sink down for further rest. Of course she was no longer than usual in completing the services assigned her. This was a subject of complaint to Mrs. Bellmont; and Frado endeavored to throw off all appearance of sickness in her presence.

But it was increasing upon her, and she could no longer hide her indisposition. Her mistress entered one day, and finding her seated, commanded her to go to work. "I am sick," replied Frado, rising and walking slowly to her unfinished task, "and cannot stand long, I feel so bad."

Angry that she should venture a reply to her command, she suddenly inflicted a blow which lay the tottering girl prostrate on the floor. Excited by so much indulgence of a dangerous passion, she seemed left to unrestrained malice; and snatching a towel, stuffed the mouth of the sufferer, and beat her cruelly.

Frado hoped she would end her misery by whipping her to death. She bore it with the hope of a martyr, that her misery would soon close. Though her mouth was muffled, and the sounds much stifled, there was a sensible commotion, which James's quick ear detected.

"Call Frado to come here," he said faintly, "I have not seen her to-day."

Susan retired with the request to the kitchen, where it was evident some brutal scene had just been enacted.

Mrs. Bellmont replied that she had "some work to do just now; when that was done, she might come."

Susan's appearance confirmed her husband's fears, and he requested his father, who sat by the bedside, to go for her. This was a messenger, as James well knew, who could not be denied; and the girl entered the room, sobbing and faint with anguish.

James called her to him, and inquired the cause of her sorrow. She was afraid to expose the cruel author of her misery, lest she should provoke new attacks. But after much entreaty, she told him all, much of which had escaped his watchful ear. Poor James shut his eyes in silence, as if pained to forgetfulness by the recital. Then turning to Susan, he asked her to take Charlie, and walk out; "she needed the fresh air," he said. "And say to my mother I wish Frado to sit by me till you return. I think you are fading, from staying so long in this sick room." Mr. B. also left, and Frado was thus left alone with her friend. Aunt Abby came in to make her daily visit, and seeing the sick countenance of the attendant, took her home with her to administer some cordial. She soon returned, however, and James kept her with him the rest of the day; and a comfortable night's repose following, she was enabled to continue, as usual, her labors. James insisted on her attending religious meetings in the vicinity with Aunt Abby.

Frado, under the instructions of Aunt Abby and the minister, became a believer in a future existence—one of happiness or misery. Her doubt was, *is* there a heaven for the black? She knew there was one for James, and Aunt Abby, and all good white people; but was there any for blacks? She had listened attentively to all the minister said, and all Aunt Abby had told her; but then it was all for white people.

As James approached that blessed world, she felt a strong desire to follow, and be with one who was such a dear, kind friend to her.

While she was exercised with these desires and aspirations, she attended an evening meeting with Aunt Abby, and the good man urged all, young or old, to accept the offers of mercy, to receive a compassionate Jesus as their Saviour. "Come to Christ," he urged, "all, young or old, white or black, bond or free, come all to Christ for pardon; repent, believe."

This was the message she longed to hear; it seemed to be spoken for her. But he had told them to repent; "what was that?" she asked. She knew she was unfit for any heaven, made for whites or blacks. She would gladly repent, or do anything which would admit her to share the abode of James.

Her anxiety increased; her countenance bore marks of solicitude unseen before; and though she said nothing of her inward contest, they all observed a change.

James and Aunt Abby hoped it was the springing of good seed sown by the Spirit of God. Her tearful attention at the last meeting encouraged his aunt to hope that her mind was awakened, her conscience aroused. Aunt Abby noticed that she was particularly engaged in reading the Bible; and this strengthened her conviction that a heavenly Messenger was striving with her. The neighbors dropped in to inquire after the sick, and also if Frado was "*serious?*" They noticed she seemed very thoughtful and tearful at the meetings. Mrs. Reed was very inquisitive; but Mrs. Bellmont saw no appearance of change for the better. She did not feel responsible for her spiritual culture, and hardly believed she had a soul.

Nig was in truth suffering much; her feelings were very intense on any subject, when once aroused. She read her Bible carefully, and as often as an opportunity presented, which was when entirely secluded in her own apartment, or by Aunt Abby's side, who kindly directed her to Christ, and instructed her in the way of salvation.

Mrs. Bellmont found her one day quietly reading her Bible. Amazed and half crediting the reports of officious neighbors, she felt it was time to interfere. Here she was, reading and shedding tears over the Bible. She ordered her to put up the book, and go to work, and not be snivelling about the house, or stop to read again.

But there was one little spot seldom penetrated by her mistress' watchful eye: this was her room, uninviting and comfortless; but to herself a safe retreat. Here she would listen to the pleadings of a Saviour, and try to penetrate the veil of doubt and sin[4] which clouded her soul, and long to cast off the fetters of sin, and rise to the communion of saints.[5]

Mrs. Bellmont, as we before said, did not trouble herself about the future destiny of her servant. If she did what she desired for *her* benefit, it was all the responsibility she acknowledged. But she seemed to have great aversion to the notice Nig would attract should she become pious. How could she meet this case? She resolved to make her complaint to John. Strange, when she was always foiled in this direction, she should resort to him. It was time something was done; she had begun to read the Bible openly.

The night of this discovery, as they were retiring, Mrs. Bellmont introduced the conversation, by saying:

"I want your attention to what I am going to say. I have let Nig go out to evening meetings a few times, and, if you will believe it, I found her reading the Bible to-day, just as though she expected to turn pious nigger, and preach to white folks. So now you see what good comes of sending her to school. If she should get converted she would have to go to meeting: at least, as long as James lives. I wish he had not such queer notions about her. It seems to trouble him to know he must die and leave her. He says if he should get well he would take her home with him, or educate her here. Oh, how awful! What can the child mean? So careful, too, of her! He says we shall ruin her health making her work so hard, and sleep in such a place. O, John! do you think he is in his right mind?"

"Yes, yes; she is slender."

"Yes, *yes!*" she repeated sarcastically, "you know these niggers are just like black snakes; you *can't* kill them. If she wasn't tough she would have been killed long ago. There was never one of my girls could do half the work."

"Did they ever try?" interposed her husband. "I think she can do more than all of them together."

"What a man!" said she, peevishly. "But I want to know what is going to be done with her about getting pious?"

"Let her do just as she has a mind to. If it is a comfort to her, let her enjoy the privilege of being good. I see no objection."

"I should think *you* were crazy, sure. Don't you know that every night she will want to go toting off to meeting? and Sundays, too? and you know we have a great deal of company Sundays, and she can't be spared."

"I thought you Christians held to going to church," remarked Mr. B.

"Yes, but who ever thought of having a nigger go, except to drive others there? Why, according to you and James, we should very soon have her in the parlor,[6] as smart as our own girls. It's of no use talking to you or James. If you should go on as you would like, it would not be six months before she would be leaving me; and that won't do. Just think how much profit she was to us last summer. We had no work hired out; she did the work of two girls—"

"And got the whippings for two with it!" remarked Mr. Bellmont.

"I'll beat the money out of her, if I can't get her worth any other way," retorted Mrs. B. sharply. While this scene was passing, Frado was trying to utter the prayer of the publican, "God be merciful to me a sinner."[7]

CHAPTER IX.

DEATH.

> We have now
> But a small portion of what men call time,
> To hold communion.[1]

Spring opened, and James, instead of rallying, as was hoped, grew worse daily. Aunt Abby and Frado were the constant allies of Susan. Mrs. Bellmont dared not lift him. She was not "strong enough," she said.

It was very offensive to Mrs. B. to have Nab about James so much. She had thrown out many a hint to detain her from so often visiting the sick-room; but Aunt Abby was too well accustomed to her ways to mind them. After various unsuccessful efforts, she resorted to the following expedient. As she heard her cross the entry below, to ascend the stairs, she slipped out and held the latch of the door which led to the upper entry.

"James does not want to see you, or any one else," she said.

Aunt Abby hesitated, and returned slowly to her own room; wondering if it were really James's wish not to see her. She did not venture again that day, but still felt disturbed and anxious about him. She inquired of Frado, and learned that he was no worse. She asked her if James did not wish her to come and see him; what could it mean?

Quite late next morning, Susan came to see what had become of her aunt.

"Your mother said James did not wish to see me, and I was afraid I tired him."

Why, aunt, that is a mistake, I *know.* What could mother mean?" asked Susan.

The next time she went to the sitting-room she asked her mother,—

"Why does not Aunt Abby visit James as she has done? Where is she?"

"At home. I hope that she will stay there," was the answer.

"I should think she would come in and see James," continued Susan.

"I told her he did not want to see her, and to stay out. You need make no stir about it; remember:" she added, with one of her fiery glances.

Susan kept silence. It was a day or two before James spoke of her absence. The family were at dinner, and Frado was watching beside him. He inquired the cause of her absence, and *she* told him all. After the family returned he sent his wife for her. When she entered, he took her hand, and said, "Come to me often, Aunt. Come any time,—I am always glad to see you. I have but a little longer to be with you,—come often, Aunt. Now please help lift me up, and see if I can rest a little."

Frado was called in, and Susan and Mrs. B. all attempted; Mrs. B. was too weak; she did not feel able to lift so much. So the three succeeded in relieving the sufferer.

Frado returned to her work. Mrs. B. followed. Seizing Frado, she said she would "cure her of tale-bearing," and, placing the wedge of wood between her teeth, she beat her cruelly with the raw-hide. Aunt Abby heard the blows, and came to see if she could hinder them.

Surprised at her sudden appearance, Mrs. B. suddenly stopped, but forbade her removing the wood till she gave her permission, and commanded Nab to go home.

She was thus tortured when Mr. Bellmont came in, and, making inquiries which she did not, because she could not, answer, approached her; and seeing her situation quickly removed the instrument of torture, and sought his wife. Their conversation we will omit; suffice it to say, a storm raged which required many days to exhaust its strength.

Frado was becoming seriously ill. She had no relish for food, and was constantly over-worked, and then she had such solicitude about the future. She wished to pray for pardon. She did try to pray. Her mistress had told her it would "do no good for her to attempt prayer; prayer was for whites, not for blacks. If she minded her mistress, and did what she commanded, it was all that was required of her."[2]

This did not satisfy her, or appease her longings. She knew her instructions did not harmonize with those of the man of God or Aunt Abby's. She resolved to persevere. She said nothing on the subject, unless asked. It was evident to all her mind was deeply exercised. James longed to speak with her alone on the subject. An opportunity presented soon, while the family were at tea. It was usual to summon Aunt Abby to keep company with her, as his death was expected hourly.

As she took her accustomed seat, he asked, "Are you afraid to stay with me alone, Frado?"

"No," she replied, and stepped to the window to conceal her emotion.

"Come here, and sit by me; I wish to talk with you."

She approached him, and, taking her hand, he remarked:

"How poor you are, Frado! I want to tell you that I fear I shall never be able to talk with you again. It is the last time, perhaps, I shall *ever* talk with you. You are old enough to remember my dying words and profit by them. I have been sick a long time; I shall die pretty soon. My Heavenly Father is calling me home. Had it been his will to let me live I should take you to live with me; but, as it is, I shall go and leave you. But, Frado, if you will be a good girl, and love and serve God, it will be but a short time before we are in a *heavenly* home together. There will never be any sickness or sorrow there."

Frado, overcome with grief, sobbed, and buried her face in his pillow. She expected he would die; but to hear him speak of his departure himself was unexpected.

"Bid me good bye, Frado."

She kissed him, and sank on her knees by his bedside; his hand rested on her head; his eyes were closed; his lips moved in prayer for this disconsolate child.

His wife entered, and interpreting the scene, gave him some restoratives, and withdrew for a short time.

It was a great effort for Frado to cease sobbing; but she dared not be seen below in tears; so she choked her grief, and descended to her usual toil. Susan perceived a change in her husband. She felt that death was near.

He tenderly looked on her, and said, "Susan, my wife, our

farewells are all spoken. I feel prepared to go. I shall meet you in heaven. Death is indeed creeping fast upon me. Let me see them all once more. Teach Charlie the way to heaven; lead him up as you come."

The family all assembled. He could not talk as he wished to them. He seemed to sink into unconsciousness. They watched him for hours. He had labored hard for breath some time, when he seemed to awake suddenly, and exclaimed, "Hark! do you hear it?"

"Hear what, my son?" asked the father.

"Their call. Look, look, at the shining ones! Oh, let me go and be at rest!"

As if waiting for this petition, the Angel of Death severed the golden thread,[3] and he was in heaven. At midnight the messenger came.

They called Frado to see his last struggle. Sinking on her knees at the foot of his bed, she buried her face in the clothes, and wept like one inconsolable. They led her from the room. She seemed to be too much absorbed to know it was necessary for her to leave. Next day she would steal into the chamber as often as she could, to weep over his remains, and ponder his last words to her. She moved about the house like an automaton. Every duty performed—but an abstraction from all, which shewed her thoughts were busied elsewhere. Susan wished her to attend his burial as one of the family. Lewis and Mary and Jack it was not thought best to send for, as the season would not allow them time for the journey. Susan provided her with a dress for the occasion, which was her first intimation that she would be allowed to mingle her grief with others.

The day of the burial she was attired in her mourning dress; but Susan, in her grief, had forgotten a bonnet.

She hastily ransacked the closets, and found one of Mary's, trimmed with bright pink ribbon.

It was too late to change the ribbon, and she was unwilling to leave Frado at home; she knew it would be the wish of James she should go with her. So tying it on, she said, "Never mind, Frado, you shall see where our dear James is buried." As she passed out, she heard the whispers of the by-standers, "Look there! see there! how that looks,—a black dress and a pink ribbon!"

Another time, such remarks would have wounded Frado. She had now a sorrow with which such were small in comparison.

As she saw his body lowered in the grave she wished to share it; but she was not fit to die. She could not go where he was if she did. She did not love God; she did not serve him or know how to.

She retired at night to mourn over her unfitness for heaven, and gaze out upon the stars, which, she felt, studded the entrance of heaven, above which James reposed in the bosom of Jesus, to which her desires were hastening. She wished she could see God, and ask him for eternal life. Aunt Abby had taught her that He was ever looking upon her. Oh, if she could see him, or hear him speak words of forgiveness. Her anxiety increased; her health seemed impaired, and she felt constrained to go to aunt Abby and tell her all about her conflicts.

She received her like a returning wanderer; seriously urged her to accept of Christ; explained the way; read to her from the Bible, and remarked upon such passages as applied to her state. She warned her against stifling that voice which was calling her to heaven; echoed the farewell words of James, and told her to come to her with her difficulties, and not to delay a duty so important as attention to the truths of religion, and her soul's interests.

Mrs. Bellmont would occasionally give instruction, though far different. She would tell her she could not go where James was; she need not try. If she should get to heaven at all, she would never be as high up as he.

He was the attraction. Should she "want to go there if she could not see him?"

Mrs. B. seldom mentioned her bereavement, unless in such allusion to Frado. She donned her weeds from custom; kept close her crape veil for so many Sabbaths, and abated nothing of her characteristic harshness.

The clergyman called to minister consolation to the afflicted widow and mother. Aunt Abby seeing him approach the dwelling, knew at once the object of his visit, and followed him to the parlor, unasked by Mrs. B! What a daring affront! The good man dispensed the consolations, of which he was steward, to the apparently grief-smitten mother, who talked like one schooled in a heavenly atmosphere. Such resignation expressed, as might have graced the trial of the holiest. Susan, like a mute sufferer, bared her soul to his sympathy and godly counsel, but only replied to his questions in short syllables. When he offered prayer, Frado stole to the door that she might hear of the heavenly bliss of one who was her friend on earth. The prayer caused profuse weeping, as any tender reminder of the heaven-born was sure to. When the good man's voice ceased, she returned to her toil, carefully removing all trace of sorrow. Her mistress soon followed, irritated by Nab's impudence in presenting herself unasked in the parlor, and upraided her with indolence, and bade her apply herself more diligently. Stung by unmerited rebuke, weak from sorrow and anxiety, the tears rolled down her dark face, soon followed by sobs, and then losing all control of herself, she wept aloud. This was an act of disobedience. Her mistress grasping her raw-hide, caused a longer flow of tears, and wounded a spirit that was craving healing mercies.

CHAPTER X.

PERPLEXITIES.— ANOTHER DEATH.

> Neath the billows of the ocean,
> Hidden treasures wait the hand,
> That again to light shall raise them
> With the diver's magic wand.
>
> G. W. Cook.[1]

The family, gathered by James's decease, returned to their homes. Susan and Charles returned to Baltimore. Letters were received from the absent, expressing their sympathy and grief. The father bowed like a "bruised reed,"[2] under the loss of his beloved son. He felt desirous to die the death of the righteous; also, conscious that he was unprepared, he resolved to start on the narrow way,[3] and some time solicit entrance through the gate which leads to the celestial city. He acknowledged his too ready acquiescence with Mrs. B., in permitting Frado to be deprived of her only religious privileges for weeks together. He accordingly asked his sister to take her to meeting once more, which she was ready at once to do.

The first opportunity they once more attended meeting together. The minister conversed faithfully with every person present. He was surprised to find the little colored girl so solicitous, and kindly directed her to the flowing fountain where she might wash and be clean. He inquired of the origin of her anxiety, of her progress up to this time, and endeavored to make Christ, instead of James, the attraction of Heaven. He invited her to come to his house, to speak freely her mind to him, to pray much, to read her Bible often.

The neighbors, who were at meeting,—among them Mrs. Reed,—discussed the opinions Mrs. Bellmont would express on the subject. Mrs. Reed called and informed Mrs. B. that her colored girl "related her experience the other night at the meeting."

"What experience?" asked she, quickly, as if she expected to hear the number of times she had whipped Frado, and the number of lashes set forth in plain Arabic numbers.

"Why, you know she is serious, don't you? She told the minister about it."

Mrs. B. made no reply, but changed the subject adroitly. Next morning she told Frado she "should not go out of the house for one while, except on errands; and if she did not stop trying to be religious, she would whip her to death."

Frado pondered; her mistress was a professor of religion; was *she* going to heaven? then she did not wish to go. If she should be near James, even, she could not be happy with those fiery eyes watching her ascending path. She resolved to give over all thought of future world, and strove daily to put her anxiety far from her.

Mr. Bellmont found himself unable to do what James or Jack could accomplish for her. He talked with her seriously, told her he had seen her many times punished undeservedly; he did not wish to have her saucy or disrespectful, but when she was *sure* she did not deserve a whipping, to avoid it if she could. "You are looking sick," he added, "you cannot endure beating as you once could."

It was not long before an opportunity offered of profiting by his advice. She was sent for wood, and not returning as soon as Mrs. B. calculated, she followed her, and, snatching from the pile a stick, raised it over her.

"Stop!" shouted Frado, "strike me, and I'll never work a mite more for you"; and throwing down what she had gathered, stood like one who feels the stirring of free and independent thoughts.

By this unexpected demonstration, her mistress, in amazement, dropped her weapon, desisting from her purpose of chastisement. Frado walked towards the house, her mistress following with the wood she herself was sent after. She did not know, before, that she had a power to ward off assaults. Her triumph in seeing her enter the door with *her* burden, repaid her for much of her former suffering.

It was characteristic of Mrs. B. never to rise in her majesty, unless she was sure she should be victorious.

This affair never met with an "after clap," like many others.

Thus passed a year. The usual amount of scolding, but fewer whippings. Mrs. B. longed once more for Mary's return, who had been absent over a year; and she wrote imperatively for her to come quickly to her. A letter came in reply, announcing that she would comply as soon as she was sufficiently recovered from an illness which detained her.

No serious apprehensions were cherished by either parent, who constantly looked for notice of her arrival, by mail. Another letter brought tidings that Mary was seriously ill; her mother's presence was solicited.

She started without delay. Before she reached her destination, a letter came to the parents announcing her death.

No sooner was the astounding news received, than Frado rushed into Aunt Abby's, exclaiming:—

"She's dead, Aunt Abby!"

"Who?" she asked, terrified by the unprefaced announcement.

"Mary; they've just had a letter."

As Mrs. B. was away, the brother and sister could freely sympathize, and she sought him in this fresh sorrow, to communicate such solace as she could, and to learn particulars of Mary's untimely death, and assist him in his journey thither.

It seemed a thanksgiving to Frado. Every hour or two she would pop into Aunt Abby's room with some strange query:

"She got into the *river* again, Aunt Abby, didn't she; the Jordan is a big one to tumble into,[4] any how. S'posen she goes to hell, she'll be as black as I am. Wouldn't mistress be mad to see her a nigger!" and others of a similar stamp, not at all acceptable to the pious, sympathetic dame; but she could not evade them.

The family returned from their sorrowful journey, leaving the dead behind. Nig looked for a change in her tyrant; what could subdue her, if the loss of her idol could not?

Never was Mrs. B. known to shed tears so profusely, as when she reiterated to one and another the sad particulars of her darling's sickness and death. There was, indeed, a season of quiet grief; it was the lull of the fiery elements. A few weeks revived the former tempests, and so at variance did they seem with chastisement sanctified, that Frado felt them to be unbearable. She determined to flee. But where? Who would take her? Mrs. B. had always represented her ugly. Perhaps every one thought her so. Then no one would take her. She was black, no one would love her. She might have to return, and then she would be more in her mistress's power than ever.

She remembered her victory at the wood-pile. She decided to remain to do as well as she could; to assert her rights when they were trampled on; to return once more to her meeting in the evening, which had been prohibited. She had learned how to conquer; she would not abuse the power while Mr. Bellmont was at home.

But had she not better run away? Where? She had never been from the place far enough to decide what course to take. She resolved to speak to Aunt Abby. *She* mapped the dangers of her course, her liability to fail in finding so good friends as John and herself. Frado's mind was busy for days and nights. She contemplated administering poison to her mistress, to rid herself and the house of so detestable a plague.[5]

But she was restrained by an overruling Providence;[6] and finally decided to stay contentedly through her period of service, which would expire when she was eighteen years of age.

In a few months Jane returned home with her family, to relieve her parents, upon whom years and affliction had left the marks of age. The years intervening since she had left her home, had, in some degree, softened the opposition to her unsanctioned marriage with George. The more Mrs. B. had about her, the more energetic seemed her directing capabilities, and her fault-finding propensities. Her own, she had full power over; and Jane after vain endeavors, became disgusted, weary, and perplexed, and decided that, though her mother might suffer, she could not endure her home. They followed Jack to the West. Thus vanished all hopes of sympathy or relief from this source to Frado. There seemed no one capable of enduring the oppression of the house but her. She turned to the darkness of the future with the determination previously formed, to remain until she should be eighteen. Jane begged her to follow her so soon as she should be released; but so wearied out was she by her mistress, she felt disposed to flee from any and every one having her similitude of name or feature.

CHAPTER XI.
MARRIAGE AGAIN.

Crucified the hopes that cheered me,
All that to the earth endeared me;
Love of wealth and fame and power,
Love,—all have been crucified.

C. E.[1]

Darkness before day. Jane left, but Jack was now to come again. After Mary's death he visited home, leaving a wife behind. An orphan whose home was with a relative, gentle, loving, the true mate of kind, generous Jack. His mother was a stranger to her, of course, and had perfect right to interrogate:

"Is she good looking, Jack?" asked his mother.

"Looks well to me," was the laconic reply.

"Was her *father* rich?"

"Not worth a copper, as I know of; I never asked him," answered Jack.

"Hadn't she any property? What did you marry her for," asked his mother.

"Oh, she's *worth a million* dollars, mother, though not a cent of it is in money."

"Jack! what do you want to bring such a poor being into the family, for? You'd better stay here, at home, and let your wife go. Why couldn't you try to do better, and not disgrace your parents?"

"Don't judge, till you see her," was Jack's reply, and immediately changed the subject. It was no recommendation to his mother, and she did not feel prepared to welcome her cordially now he was to come with his wife. He was indignant at his mother's advice to desert her. It rankled bitterly in his soul, the bare suggestion. He had more to bring. He now came with a child also. He decided to leave the West, but not his family.

Upon their arrival, Mrs. B. extended a cold welcome to her new daughter, eyeing her dress with closest scrutiny. Poverty was to her a disgrace, and she could not associate with any thus dishonored. This coldness was felt by Jack's worthy wife, who only strove the harder to recommend herself by her obliging, winning ways.

Mrs. B. could never let Jack be with her alone without complaining of this or that deficiency in his wife.

He cared not so long as the complaints were piercing his own ears. He would not have Jenny[2] disquieted. He passed his time in seeking employment.

A letter came from his brother Lewis, then at the South, soliciting his services. Leaving his wife, he repaired thither.

Mrs. B. felt that great restraint was removed, that Jenny was more in her own power. She wished to make her feel her inferiority; to relieve Jack of his burden if he would not do it himself. She watched her incessantly, to catch at some act of Jenny's which might be construed into conjugal unfaithfulness.

Near by were a family of cousins, one a young man of Jack's age, who, from love to his cousin, proffered all needful courtesy to his stranger relative. Soon news reached Jack that Jenny was deserting her covenant vows, and had formed an illegal intimacy with his cousin. Meantime Jenny was told by her mother-in-law that Jack did not marry her untrammelled. He had another love whom he would be glad, even now, if he could, to marry. It was very doubtful if he ever came for her.

Jenny would feel pained by her unwelcome gossip, and, glancing at her child, she decided, however true it might be, she had a pledge which would enchain him yet. Ere long, the mother's inveterate hate crept out into some neighbor's enclosure, and, caught up hastily, they passed the secret round till it became none, and Lewis was sent for, the brother by whom Jack was employed. The neighbors saw her fade in health and spirits; they found letters never reached their destination when sent by either. Lewis arrived with the joyful news that he had come to take Jenny home with him.

What a relief to her to be freed from the gnawing taunts of her adversary.

Jenny retired to prepare for the journey, and Mrs. B. and Lewis had a long interview. Next morning he informed Jenny that new clothes would be necessary, in order to make her presentable to Baltimore society, and he should return without her, and she must stay till she was suitably attired.

Disheartened, she rushed to her room, and, after relief from weeping, wrote to Jack to come; to have pity on her, and take her to him. No answer came. Mrs. Smith,[3] a neighbor, watchful and friendly, suggested that she write away from home, and employ some one to carry it to the office who would elude Mrs. B., who, they very well knew, had intercepted Jenny's letter, and influenced Lewis to leave her behind. She accepted the offer, and Frado succeeded in managing the affair so that Jack soon came to the rescue, angry, wounded, and forever after alienated from his early home and his mother. Many times would Frado steal up into Jenny's room, when she knew she was tortured by her mistress' malignity, and tell some of her own encounters with her, and tell her she might "be sure it wouldn't kill her, for she should have died long before at the same treatment."

Susan and her child succeeded Jenny as visitors. Frado had merged into womanhood, and, retaining what she had learned, in spite of the few privileges enjoyed formerly, was striving to enrich her mind. Her school-books were her constant companions, and every leisure moment was applied to them. Susan was delighted to witness her progress, and some little book from her was a reward sufficient for any task imposed, however difficult. She had her book always fastened open near her, where she could glance from toil to soul refreshment. The approaching spring would close the term of years which Mrs. B. claimed as the period of her servitude. Often as she passed the waymarks of former years did she pause to ponder on her situation, and wonder if she *could* succeed in providing for her own wants. Her health was delicate, yet she resolved to try.

Soon she counted the time by days which should release her. Mrs. B. felt that she could not well spare one who could so well adapt herself to all departments—man, boy, housekeeper, domestic, etc. She begged Mrs. Smith to talk with her, to show her how ungrateful it would appear to leave a home of such comfort—how wicked it was to be ungrateful! But Frado replied that she had had enough of such comforts; she wanted some new ones; and as it was so wicked to be ungrateful, she would go from temptation; Aunt Abby said "we mustn't put ourselves in the way of temptation."

Poor little Fido! She shed more tears over him than over all beside.

The morning for departure dawned. Frado engaged to work for a family a mile distant. Mrs. Bellmont dismissed her with the assurance that she would soon wish herself back again, and a present of a silver half dollar.

Her wardrobe consisted of one decent dress, without any superfluous accompaniments. A Bible from Susan she felt was her greatest treasure.

Now was she alone in the world. The past year had been one of suffering resulting from a fall, which had left her lame.

The first summer passed pleasantly, and the wages earned were expended in garments necessary for health and cleanliness. Though feeble, she was well satisfied with her progress. Shut up in her room, after her toil was finished, she studied what poor samples of apparel she had, and, for the first time, prepared her own garments.

Mrs. Moore,[4] who employed her, was a kind friend to her, and attempted to heal her wounded spirit by sympathy and advice, burying the past in the prospects of the future. But her failing health was a cloud no kindly human hand could dissipate. A little light work was all she could accomplish. A clergyman, whose family was small, sought her, and she was removed there. Her engagement with Mrs. Moore finished in the fall. Frado was anxious to keep up her reputation for efficiency, and often pressed far beyond prudence. In the winter she entirely gave up work, and confessed herself thoroughly sick. Mrs. Hale,[5] soon overcome by additional cares, was taken sick also, and now it became necessary to adopt some measures for Frado's comfort, as well as to relieve Mrs. Hale. Such dark forebodings as visited her as she lay, solitary and sad, no moans or sighs could relieve.

The family physician pronounced her case one of doubtful issue. Frado hoped it was final. She could not feel relentings that her former home was abandoned, and yet, should she be in need of succor could she obtain it from one who would now so grudgingly bestow it? The family were applied to, and it was decided to take her there. She was removed to a room built out from the main building, used formerly as a workshop, where cold and rain found unobstructed access, and here she fought with bitter reminiscences and future prospects till she became reckless of her faith and hopes and person, and half wished to end what nature seemed so tardily to take.

Aunt Abby made her frequent visits, and at last had her removed to her own apartment, where she might supply her wants, and minister to her once more in heavenly things.

Then came the family consultation.

"What is to be done with her," asked Mrs. B., "after she is moved there with Nab?"

"Send for the Dr., your brother," Mr. B. replied.

"When?"

"To-night."

"To-night! and for her! Wait till morning," she continued.

"She has waited too long now; I think something should be done soon."

"I doubt if she is much sick," sharply interrupted Mrs. B.

"Well, we'll see what our brother thinks."

His coming was longed for by Frado, who had known him well during her long sojourn in the family; and his praise of her nice butter and cheese, from which his table was supplied, she knew he felt as well as spoke.

"You're sick, very sick," he said, quickly, after a moment's pause. "Take good care of her, Abby, or she'll never get well. All broken down."

"Yes, it was at Mrs. Moore's," said Mrs. B., "all this was done. She did but little the latter part of the time she was here."

"It was commenced longer ago than last summer. Take good care of her; she may never get well," remarked the Dr.

"We sha'n't pay you for doctoring her; you may look to the town for that, sir," said Mrs. B., and abruptly left the room.

"Oh dear! oh dear!" exclaimed Frado, and buried her face in the pillow.

A few kind words of consolation, and she was once more alone in the darkness which enveloped her previous days. Yet she felt sure they owed her a shelter and attention, when disabled, and she resolved to feel patient, and remain till she could help herself. Mrs. B. would not attend her, nor permit her domestic to stay with her at all. Aunt Abby was her sole comforter. Aunt Abby's nursing had the desired effect, and she slowly improved. As soon as she was able to be moved, the kind Mrs. Moore took her to her home again, and completed what Aunt Abby had so well commenced. Not that she was well, or ever would be; but she had recovered so far as rendered it hopeful she might provide for her own wants. The clergyman at whose house she was taken sick, was now seeking some one to watch his sick children, and as soon as he heard of her recovery, again asked for her services.

What seemed so light and easy to others, was too much for Frado; and it became necessary to ask once more where the sick should find an asylum.

All felt that the place where her declining health began, should be the place of relief; so they applied once more for a shelter.

"No," exclaimed the indignant Mrs. B.; "she shall never come under this roof again; never! never!" she repeated, as if each repetition were a bolt to prevent admission.

One only resource; the public must pay the expense. So she was removed to the home of two maidens, (old,) who had principle enough to be willing to earn the money a charitable public disburses.

Three years of weary sickness wasted her, without extinguishing a life apparently so feeble. Two years had these maidens watched and cared for her, and they began to weary, and finally to request the authorities to remove her.

Mrs. Hoggs[6] was a lover of gold and silver, and she asked the favor of filing her coffers by caring for the sick. The removal caused severe sickness.

By being bolstered in the bed, after a time she could use her hands, and often would ask for sewing to beguile the tedium. She had become very expert with her needle the first year of her release from Mrs. B., and she had forgotten none of her skill. Mrs. H. praised her, and as she improved in health, was anxious to employ her. She told her she could in this way replace her clothes, and as her board would be paid for, she would thus gain something.

Many times her hands wrought when her body was in pain; but the hope that she might yet help herself, impelled her on.

Thus she reckoned her store of means by a few dollars, and was hoping soon to come in possession, when she was startled by the announcement that Mrs. Hoggs had reported her to the physician and town offices as an impostor. That she was, in truth, able to get up and go to work.

This brought on a severe sickness of two weeks, when Mrs. Moore again sought her, and took her to her home. She had formerly had wealth at her command, but misfortune had deprived her of it, and unlocked her heart to sympathies and favors she had never known while it lasted. Her husband, defrauded of his last means by a branch of the Bellmont family, had supported them by manual labor, gone to the West, and left his wife and four young children. But she felt humanity required her to give a shelter to one she knew to be worthy of a hospitable reception. Mrs. Moore's physician was called, and pronounced her a very sick girl, and encouraged Mrs. M. to keep her and care for her, and he would see that the authorities were informed of Frado's helplessness, and pledged assistance.

Here she remained till sufficiently restored to sew again. Then came the old resolution to take care of herself, to cast off the unpleasant charities of the public.

She learned that in some towns in Massachusetts, girls make straw bonnets—that it was easy and profitable. But how should *she,* black, feeble and poor, find any one to teach her. But God prepares the way, when human agencies see no path. Here was found a plain, poor, simple woman, who could see merit beneath a dark skin; and when the invalid mulatto told her sorrows, she opened her door and her heart, and took the stranger in. Expert with the needle, Frado soon equalled her instructress;

and she sought also to teach her the value of useful books; and while one read aloud to the other of deeds historic and names renowned, Frado experienced a new impulse. She felt herself capable of elevation; she felt that this book information supplied an undefined dissatisfaction she had long felt, but could not express. Every leisure moment was carefully applied to self-improvement, and a devout and Christian exterior invited confidence from the villagers. Thus she passed months of quiet, growing in the confidence of her neighbors and new found friends.

CHAPTER XII.
THE WINDING UP OF THE MATTER.

Nothing new under the sun.
SOLOMON.[1]

A few years ago, within the compass of my narrative,[2] there appeared often in some of our New England villages, professed fugitives[3] from slavery, who recounted their personal experience in homely phrase, and awakened the indignation of non-slaveholders against brother Pro. Such a one appeared in the new home of Frado; and as people of color were rare there, was it strange she should attract her dark brother; that he should inquire her out; succeed in seeing her; feel a strange sensation in his heart towards her; that he should toy with her shining curls, feel proud to provoke her to smile and expose the ivory concealed by thin, ruby lips; that her sparkling eyes should fascinate; that he should propose; that they should marry? A short acquaintance was indeed an objection, but she saw him often, and thought she knew him. He never spoke of his enslavement to her when alone, but she felt that, like her own oppression, it was painful to disturb oftener than was needful.

He was a fine, straight negro, whose back showed no marks of the lash, erect as if it never crouched beneath a burden. There was a silent sympathy which Frado felt attracted her, and she opened her heart to the presence of love—that arbitrary and inexorable tyrant.

She removed to Singleton, her former residence, and there was married. Here were Frado's first feelings of trust and repose on human arm. She realized, for the first time, the relief of looking to another for comfortable support. Occasionally he would leave her to "lecture."

Those tours were prolonged often to weeks. Of course he had little spare money. Frado was again feeling her self-dependence, and was at last compelled to resort alone to that. Samuel was kind to her when at home, but made no provision for his absence,[4] which was at last unprecedented.

He left her to her fate—embarked at sea, with the disclosure that he had never seen the South, and that his illiterate harangues were humbugs for hungry abolitionists.[5] Once more alone! Yet not alone. A still newer companionship would soon force itself upon her. No one wanted her with such prospects. Herself was burden enough; who would have an additional one?

The horrors of her condition nearly prostrated her, and she was again thrown upon the public for sustenance. Then followed the birth of her child.[6] The long absent Samuel unexpectedly returned, and rescued her from charity. Recovering from her expected illness, she once more commenced toil for herself and child, in a room obtained of a poor woman, but with better fortune. One so well known would not be wholly neglected. Kind friends watched her when Samuel was from home, prevented her from suffering, and when the cold weather pinched the warmly clad, a kind friend took them in, and thus preserved them. At last Samuel's business became very engrossing, and after long desertion, news reached his family that he had become a victim of yellow fever, in New Orleans.

So much toil as was necessary to sustain Frado, was more than she could endure. As soon as her babe could be nourished without his mother, she left him in charge[7] of a Mrs. Capon,[8] and procured an agency, hoping to recruit her health, and gain an easier livelihood for herself and child. This afforded her better maintenance than she had yet found. She passed into the various towns of the State she lived in, then into Massachusetts. Strange were some of her adventures. Watched by kidnappers,[9] maltreated by professed abolitionists,[10] who didn't want slaves at the South, nor niggers in their own houses, North. Faugh! to lodge one; to eat with one; to admit one through the front door; to sit next one; awful!

Traps slyly laid by the vicious to ensnare her,[11] she resolutely avoided. In one of her tours, Providence favored her with a friend who, pitying her cheerless lot, kindly provided her with a valuable recipe, from which she might herself manufacture a useful article for her maintenance. This proved a more agreeable, and easier way of sustenance.

And thus, to the present time, may you see her busily employed in preparing her merchandise; then sallying forth to encounter many frowns, but some kind friends and purchasers. Nothing turns her from her steadfast purpose of elevating herself. Reposing on God, she has thus far journeyed securely. Still an invalid, she asks your sympathy, gentle reader.[12] Refuse not, because some part of her history is unknown, save by the Omniscient God. Enough has been unrolled to demand your sympathy and aid.

Do you ask the destiny of those connected with her *early* history? A few years only have elapsed since Mr. and Mrs. B. passed into another world. As age increased, Mrs. B. became more irritable, so that no one, even her own children, could remain with her; and she was accompanied by her husband to the home of Lewis, where, after an agony in death unspeakable, she passed away. Only a few months since, Aunt Abby entered heaven. Jack and his wife rest in heaven, disturbed by no intruders; and Susan and her child are yet with the living. Jane has silver locks in place of auburn tresses, but she has the early love of George still, and has never regretted her exchange of lovers. Frado has passed from their memories, as Joseph from the butler's, but she will never cease to track them till beyond mortal vision.[13]

APPENDIX.

"Truth is stranger than fiction;" and whoever reads the narrative of Alfrado, will find the assertion verified.

About eight years ago I became acquainted with the author of this book, and I feel it a privilege to speak a few words in her behalf. Through the instrumentality of an itinerant colored lecturer,[1] she was brought to W——, Mass. This is an ancient town, where the mothers and daughters seek, not "wool and flax," but *straw,*—working willingly with their hands! Here she was introduced to the family of Mrs. Walker,[2] who kindly consented to receive her as an inmate of her household, and immediately succeeded in procuring work for her as a "straw sewer." Being very ingenious, she soon acquired the art of making hats; but on account of former hard treatment, her constitution was greatly impaired, and she was subject to seasons of sickness. On this account Mrs. W. gave her a room joining her own chamber, where she could hear her faintest call. Never shall I forget the expression of her "black, but comely"[3] face, as she came to me one day, exclaiming, "O, aunt J——, I have at last found a *home,*—and not only a home, but a *mother.* My cup runneth over.[4] What shall I render to the Lord for all his benefits?"

Months passed on, and she was *happy*—truly happy. Her health began to improve under the genial sunshine in which she lived, and she even looked forward with *hope*—joyful hope to the future. But, alas, "it is not in man that walketh to direct his steps."[5] One beautiful morning in the early spring of 1842, as she was taking her usual walk, she chanced to meet her old friend, the "lecturer," who brought her to W——, and with him was a fugitive slave. Young, well-formed and very handsome, he said he had been a *house*-servant, which seemed to account in some measure for his gentlemanly manners and pleasing address. The meeting was entirely accidental; but it was a sad occurrence for poor Alfrado, as her own sequel tells. Suffice it to say, an acquaintance and attachment was formed, which, in due time, resulted in marriage. In a few days she left W——, and *all* her home comforts, and took up her abode in New Hampshire. For a while everything went on well, and she dreamed not of danger; but in an evil hour he left his young and trusting wife, and embarked for sea. She knew nothing of all this, and waited for his return. But she waited in vain. Days passed, weeks passed, and he came not; then her heart failed her. She felt herself deserted at a time, when, of all others, she most needed the care and soothing attentions of a devoted husband. For a time she tried to sustain *herself,* but this was impossible. She had friends, but they were mostly of that class who are poor in the things of earth, but "rich in faith."[6] The charity on which she depended failed at last, and there was nothing to save her from the "County House;"[7] *go she must.* But her feelings on her way thither, and after her arrival, can be given better in her own language; and I trust it will be no breach of confidence if I here insert part of a letter she wrote her mother Walker, concerning the matter.

"The evening before I left for my dreaded journey to the 'house' which was to be my abode, I packed my trunk, carefully placing it in every little memento of affection received from *you* and my friends in W——, among which was the portable inkstand, pens and paper. My beautiful little Bible was laid aside, as a place nearer my heart was reserved for that. I need not tell you I slept not a moment that night. My home, my peaceful, quiet home with you, was before me. I could see my dear little room, with its pleasant eastern window opening to the morning; but more than all, I beheld *you,* my mother, gliding softly in and kneeling by my bed to read, as no one but you *can* read, 'The Lord is my shepherd,—I shall not want.' But I cannot go on, for tears blind me. For a description of the morning, and of the scant breakfast, I must wait until another time.

"We started. The man who came for me was kind as he could

be,—helped me carefully into the wagon, (for I had no strength,) and drove on. For miles I spoke not a word. Then the silence would be broken by the driver uttering some sort of word the horse seemed to understand; for he invariably quickened his pace. And so, just before nightfall, we halted at the institution, prepared for the *homeless*. With cold civility the matron received me, and bade one of the inmates shew me my room. She did so; and I followed up two flights of stairs. I crept as I was able; and when she said, 'Go in there,' I obeyed, asking for my trunk, which was soon placed by me. My room was furnished some like the 'prophet's chamber,' except there was no 'candlestick';[8] so when I could creep down I begged for a light, and it was granted. Then I flung myself on the bed and cried, until I could cry no longer. I rose up and tried to pray; the Saviour seemed near. I opened my precious little Bible, and the first verse that caught my eye was—'I am poor and needy,[9] yet the Lord thinketh upon me.' O, my mother, could I tell you the comfort this was to me. I sat down, calm, almost happy, took my pen and wrote on the inspiration of the moment—

"O, holy Father, by thy power,
Thus far in life I'm brought;
And now in this dark, trying hour,
O God, forsake me not.

"Dids't thou not nourish and sustain
My infancy and youth?
Have I not testimonials plain,
Of thy unchanging truth?

"Though I've no home to call my own,
My heart shall not repine;
The saint may live on earth unknown,
And yet in glory shine.

"When my Redeemer dwelt below,
He chose a lowly lot;
He came unto his own, but lo!
His own received him not.

"Oft was the mountain his abode,
The cold, cold earth his bed;
The midnight moon shone softly down
On his unsheltered head.

"But *my* head *was sheltered,* and I tried to feel thankful."

Two or three letters were received after this by her friends in W——, and then all was silent. No one of us knew whether she still lived or had gone to her home on high. But it seems she remained in this house until after the birth of her babe; then her faithless husband returned, and took her to some town in New Hampshire, where, for a time, he supported her and his little son decently well. But again he left her as before—suddenly and unexpectedly, and she saw him no more. Her efforts were again successful in a measure in securing a meagre maintenance for a time; but her struggles with poverty and sickness were severe. At length, a door of hope was opened. A kind gentleman and lady[10] took her little boy into their own family, and provided everything necessary for his good; and all this without the hope of remuneration. But let them know, they shall be "recompensed at the resurrection of the just."[11] God is not unmindful of this work,—this labor of love. As for the afflicted mother, she too has been remembered. The heart of a stranger was moved with compassion, and bestowed a recipe upon her for restoring gray hair to its former color.[12] She availed herself of this great help, and has been quite successful; but her health is again failing, and she has felt herself obliged to resort to another method of procuring her bread—that of writing an Autobiography.[13]

I trust she will find a ready sale for her interesting work; and let all the friends who purchase a volume, remember they are doing good to one of the most worthy, and I had almost said most unfortunate, of the human family. I will only add in conclusion, a few lines, calculated to comfort and strengthen this sorrowful, homeless one. "I will help thee, saith the Lord."[14]

"I will help thee," promise kind,
Made by our High Priest above;
Soothing to the troubled mind,
Full of tenderness and love.

"I will help thee" when the storm
Gathers dark on every side;
Safely from impending harm,
In my sheltering bosom hide.

"I will help thee," weary saint,
Cast thy burdens *all on me;*
Oh, how cans't thou tire or faint,
While my arm circles thee.

I have pitied every tear,
Heard and *counted* every sigh;
Ever lend a gracious ear
To thy supplicating cry.

What though thy wounded bosom bleed,
Pierced by affliction's dart;
Do I not all thy sorrows heed,
And bear thee on my heart?

Soon will the lowly grave become
Thy quiet resting place;
Thy spirit find a peaceful home
In mansions *near my face.*

There are thy robes and glittering crown,
Outshining yonder sun;
Soon shalt thou lay the body down,
And put those glories on.

Long has thy golden lyre been strung,
    Which angels cannot move;
No song to this is ever sung,
    But bleeding, dying Love.

ALLIDA.[15]

TO THE FRIENDS OF OUR DARK-COMPLEXIONED BRETHREN AND SISTERS, THIS NOTE IS INTENDED.

Having known the writer of this book for a number of years, and knowing the many privations and mortifications she has had to pass through, I the more willingly add my testimony to the truth of her assertions. She is one of that class, who by some are considered not only as little lower than the angels, but far beneath them; but I have long since learned that we are not to look at the color of the hair, the eyes, or the skin, for the man or woman; their life is the criterion we are to judge by. The writer of this book has seemed to be a child of misfortune.

Early in life she was deprived of her parents, and all those endearing associations to which childhood clings. Indeed, she may be said not to have had that happy period; for, being taken from home so young, and placed where she had nothing to love or cling to, I often wonder she had not grown up a *monster;* and those very people calling themselves Christians, (the good Lord deliver me from such,) and they likewise ruined her health by hard work, both in the field and house. She was indeed a slave, in every sense of the word;[16] and a lonely one, too.[17]

But she has found some friends in this degraded world, that were willing to do by others as they would have others do by them; that were willing she should live, and have an existence on the earth with them. She has never enjoyed any degree of comfortable health since she was eighteen years of age, and a great deal of the time has been confined to her room and bed. She is now trying to write a book; and I hope the public will look favorably on it, and patronize the same, for she is a worthy woman.

Her own health being poor, and having a child to care for,

(for, by the way, she has been married,) and she wishes to educate him; in her sickness he has been taken from her, and sent to the county farm, because she could not pay his board every week; but as soon as she was able, she took him from that *place,* and now he has a home where he is considered as good as those he is with. He is an intelligent, smart boy, and no doubt will make a smart man, if he is rightly managed. He is beloved by his playmates, and by all the friends of the family; for the family do not recognize those as friends who do not include him in their family, or as one of them, and his mother as a daughter—for they treat her as such; and she certainly deserves all the affection and kindness that is bestowed upon her, and they are always happy to have her visit them whenever she will. They are not wealthy, but the latch-string is always out when suffering humanity needs a shelter; the last loaf they are willing to divide with those more needy than themselves, remembering these words, Do good as we have opportunity; and we can always find opportunity, if we have the disposition.

And now I would say, I hope those who call themselves friends of our dark-skinned brethren, will lend a helping hand, and assist our sister, not in giving, but in buying a book; the expense is trifling, and the reward of doing good is great. Our duty is to our fellow-beings, and when we let an opportunity pass, we know not what we lose. Therefore we should do with all our might what our hands find to do; and remember the words of Him who went about doing good, that inasmuch as ye have done a good deed[18] to one of the least of these my brethren, ye have done it to me; and even a cup of water is not forgotten. Therefore, let us work while the day lasts, and we shall in no wise lose our reward.[19]

MARGARETTA THORN.[20]

MILFORD, JULY 20TH, 1859.

Feeling a deep interest in the welfare of the writer of this book, and hoping that its circulation will be extensive, I wish to say a few words in her behalf. I have been acquainted with her for several years, and have always found her worthy the esteem of all friends of humanity; one whose soul is alive to the work to which she puts her hand. Although her complexion is a little darker than my own, I esteem it a privilege to associate with her, and assist her whenever an opportunity presents itself. It is with this motive that I write these few lines, knowing this book must be interesting to all who have any knowledge of the writer's character, or wish to have. I hope no one will refuse to aid her in her work, as she is worthy the sympathy of all Christians, and those who have a spark of humanity in their breasts.

Thinking it unnecessary for me to write a long epistle, I will close by bidding her God speed.

C. D. S.[21]

Documents from the Life of Harriet E. Wilson

Mrs. H. E. Wilson's "Hair Dressing" and "Hair Regenerator" bottles. By 1860, Henry P. Wilson was marketing and manufacturing her products. *(Collection of Pier Gabrielle Foreman. By permission.)*

"USE THE BEST!"

MRS. WILSON'S HAIR REGENERATOR.

The Regenerator is put up in two sizes, and retails for 50 cents for pint bottles, and $1 for quart bottles. The quart bottles are much the cheapest.

Who wants a Good Head of Hair? Use Mrs. Wilson's Hair Regenerator and Hair Dressing.

Please read a few certificates from the following reliable and well known people.

MESSRS. HENRY P. WILSON & CO.—My wife is now using your Regenerator for the hair, and pronounces it far superior to anything she ever used for the hair. It is easily applied, does not soil in the least—has no disagreeable odor, increases the growth of hair, prevents it falling off, and often cures the headache. I forward you this certificate unsolicited, because I think an article that will do what your Hair Regenerator will, should be widely known. I think it is the best article for the hair now in use. *Respectfully, &c.,*

REV. JACOB STEVENS, Newburyport, Ms.

"*I like the Hair Regenerator and Dressing very much.*" REV. GEO. W. WOODING, Hartford, Ct.

"*I unhesitatingly pronounce it an invaluable article from the effect on my own head.*"
S. A. HILL, wife of Rev. Henry Hill, Manchester, N. H.

"*It rendered my hair soft and glossy.*"
MINOT FARRAR, Saratoga Springs, N. Y.

"*I feel confident that it operates* NOT *as a dye, but to restore the roots to their natural healthy state.*"
REV. E. M. KELLOG, Nashua, N. H.

"*I most cheerfully recommend it to all persons.*"
REV. C. RUSSELL, Littleton, N. H.

November 1.

MESSRS. HENRY P. WILSON & CO.: I have no hesitancy in saying, in my opinion, Mrs. Wilson's Hair Regenerator and Hair Dressing are the best hair preparations now in use. I shall continue to use them with pleasure.

REV. H. H. HARTWELL, Lawrence, Mass.

November.

MESSRS. HENRY P. WILSON & CO.: I have used your Hair Regenerator and Hair Dressing, and have received great benefit from them. I deem the articles worthy of high commendation, and cheerfully recommend them to all who want to restore gray hair to its original color, or to any who are troubled with dandruff, or a disagreeable itching of the head, or humors, or to those whose hair is falling from the head.

REV. G. W. H. CLARK, Great Falls, N. H.

MESSRS. HENRY P. WILSON & CO.: I deem Mrs. Wilson's Hair Regenerator and Hair Dressing the standard articles of all hair preparations. I have, in many instances, known them to restore the hair where it had fallen off, remove dandruff, restore the hair to its original color, cure entirely the most painful headaches—and in some instances most serious humors Personally, I have been a sharer in several of these benefits.

REV. HENRY HILL, Manchester, N. H.

MRS. WILSON'S COCOA-NUT OIL HAIR DRESSING.

Mrs. Wilson's Hair Dressing is put up in large bottles, and retails for 37 cts. per bottle, and for dressing the hair of any person, young or old, there is not its equal in the world. It will make the hair everything you wish it to be, and moreover, it has a perfume that is infinitely superior to any of the fashionable extracts, either foreign or American, which alone should entitle it to a place on every lady's toilet table.

Use the Regenerator before retiring at night, and in the morning apply a little of the Dressing, and your hair will be even more lifelike in color and beauty.

Use nothing on your hair but these preparations, and use these according to directions, and we warrant you a good healthy head of hair.

Manufactured and sold at wholesale by Henry P. Wilson & Co., Manchester, N. H., to whom all letters should be addressed.

Sold in Lowell by SAMUEL KIDDER, JR., and CARLETON & HOVEY.

Wholesale Agents, G. C. Goodwin and M. S. Burr, Boston. aug20*3tawly

The featured image matches remnants of an image found on the very rare Mrs. H. E. Wilson hairdressing bottles with partial labels (in the collection of P. Gabrielle Foreman). This advertisement appeared in papers in cities from Connecticut to New Jersey. By 1860, Henry P. Wilson (no relation) was manufacturing and marketing the products that bear Mrs. H. E. Wilson's name. *(From Gale. 19th Century U.S. Newspapers. © 2008 Gale, a part of Cengage Learning, Inc. Reproduced by permission. www.cengage.com/permissions.)*

Who wants a Good Head of Hair?

MRS. WILSON'S

HAIR REGENERATOR

Is believed to be the best preoaration for the Hair ever made. It frees the bead from dandruff, and heals it of humors, restores the hair to its natural color, and reproduces it where it has fallen off.

IT IS NO HUMBUG! TRY IT & SEE!

PREPARED BY MRS. H. E. WILSON,

32-1y* No. 9 Winter street, Nashua.

Advertisement from the *Farmer's Cabinet* (Amherst, New Hampshire), January 19, 1859, 4. *(From Early American Newspapers, an Archive of Americana Collection, published by Readex [Readex.com], a division of NewsBank, and in cooperation with the American Antiquarian Society. Reprinted by permission.)*

(Copy sent)

FORM C.

Commonwealth of Massachusetts.

No. 192

RETURN OF A DEATH.

To the Clerk of the City or Town in which the death occurred.

(FILL OUT WITH INK. ALL NAMES TO BE IN FULL.)

Name, Hattie E. Wilson Sex, F Color, African

Date of Death, June 28 1900; Age, 75 Years, 3 Months, 13 Days.

Maiden Name, (If married, widowed or divorced.) Hattie E. Green

Husband's Name, —

~~Single, Married~~, Widowed ~~or Divorced~~, Occupation, Nurse

*Residence, (If out of town, also state fully.) Boston Mass. 9 Pelham St.

Place of Birth, Milford N.H.

*Place of Death, Quincy Mass. 93 Washington St.

Name and Birthplace of Father, Joshua Green —

Maiden Name and Birthplace of Mother, —

Place of Interment, (Give name of Cemetery), Quincy Mass. Mt. Wollaston

Dated at Quincy Mass. on June 1900

Signature and place of business of Undertaker. John Hall 90 Hancock St. Quincy

PHYSICIAN'S CERTIFICATE.

Name and Age of Deceased,† Hattie E. Wilson Age, 75 Y. 3 M. 13 D.

Place and Date of Death, died at Quincy 93 Washington St. June 28 1900.

Disease or Cause of Death,‡ Primary, Inanition Duration, two months

Secondary, incident to old age. Duration,

I certify that the above is true to the best of my knowledge and belief.

Signature and Residence of Certifying Physician. C. W. Garey M. D. "198 Hancock St.

Date of Certificate, June 29 1900.

*Give also street and number, if any. † Give sex of infant not named. If still-born, so state. ‡ If a Soldier or Sailor in the War of the Rebellion, give both Primary and Secondary Cause.

Board of Health, the board or agent shall forthwith countersign and transmit the same to the clerk of the city or town for registration.

Countersign and transmit to the clerk of the city or town.

Agent of Board of Health.

"Return of a Death" for Hattie E. Wilson, June 29, 1900 (date of death, June 28). The certificate shows that Wilson, who resided in Boston, was born in Milford, New Hampshire, in March 1825.

Explanatory Notes

TITLE PAGE AND PREFACE

1. *Sketches from the Life of a Free Black: Our Nig*'s subtitle recalls narratives such as *Narrative of the Life of Frederick Douglass, an American Slave* (1845) and anticipates Harriet Jacobs's *Incidents in the Life of a Slave Girl* (1861). On its cover page, however, "our nig" remains both nameless and genderless, a mere possession. By announcing that the narrative is written "by 'our Nig,'" Wilson both underscores her dispossession while she also challenges it. As Henry Louis Gates, Jr. noted, through the title, Wilson offers ironic commentary on black authorship and ownership. See Henry Louis Gates, Jr. introduction to *Our Nig* (New York: Vintage Books, 1983), li.
2. *Two-Story White House, North:* In addition to the obvious reference to the national implications of Wilson's story conveyed in the reference to the White House, this phrase cues the reader to be attentive to the multiple stories told in *Our Nig,* the fact that the text itself tells at least two stories.
3. *"giving assault to all—Holland":* Josiah Gilbert Holland, "Bittersweet: A Poem," in *Bittersweet,* 5th ed. (New York: Charles Scribner, 1959), 35–36. There are minor differences between Wilson's epigraphs and the actual sources. Wilson repeatedly slightly misquotes or changes punctuation in epigraphs, suggesting that she may be quoting them from memory. (From note compiled by Henry Louis Gates, Jr. and R. J. Ellis as found in *Our Nig,* 3rd ed. [New York: Vintage Books, 2002]. Notes on all epigraphs come from this source, unless otherwise noted.)
4. *Geo. C. Rand & Avery:* The two principals in this Boston publishing company were George C. Rand, who was a personal friend of and worked closely with abolitionist William Lloyd Garrison, and Abraham Avery, his brother-in-law. Suggestively, Geo C. Rand

& Avery also published Spiritualist titles; and it is likely that Wilson was beginning to connect with the Spiritualist community at the time she published *Our Nig*. Eric Gardner found that William Lloyd Garrison, Jr. possessed a copy of *Our Nig* at his death and notes that the connection between Rand and Garrison, Sr. may explain this. Garrison, along with many other prominent abolitionists and women's rights activists, also had strong links with Spiritualists. See Florence Osgood Rand, *A Genealogy of the Rand Family in the United States* (New York: Republic Press, 1898); R. J. Ellis, *Harriet Wilson's "Our Nig"* (Amsterdam: Rodopi Press, 2003), 27; Eric Gardner, " 'This Attempt of Their Sister': Harriet Wilson's *Our Nig* from Printer to Reader," *New England Quarterly* 66, no. 2 (June 1993): 226–46; Ann Braude, *Radical Spirits: Spiritualism and Women's Rights in Nineteenth-Century America* (Bloomington: Indiana University Press, 2001), 73.

5. *maintaining myself and child:* Antebellum women writers, black and nonblack, often felt the need to justify their step into public arenas. Economic hardship and the necessary support of their families were seen as acceptable reasons to do so, while self-expression or the desire to impact public opinion were seen as decidedly unfeminine and unacceptable. Many women writers took on pen names or used their initials to shield themselves from the gendered implications and informal restrictions on their public interventions. Sarah L. Forten (Ada), Harriet Jacobs (Linda Brent), the biographer "Frank" (Frances) Rollin, and Mrs. A. E. Johnson are among the nineteenth-century black women writers whose authorial practices reflect this dynamic.
6. *anti-slavery friends at home:* "Anti-slavery friends" is a common term, seen in newspapers, letters, and addresses within the abolitionist movement. Wilson's ironic usage displays her familiarity with such rhetoric. Milford, her "at home," was associated with some of the strongest abolitionist activities in New Hampshire; the story she tells, as well as what she "omits," would, she asserts, provoke shame for its residents, many of whom considered themselves to be true friends of freedom.
7. *confession of errors:* Wilson modifies the standard "apologia" that is so often a part of novelistic and narrative prefaces regardless of the author's educational background or racial or gender identity.
8. *appeal to my colored brethren:* While no reviews or extant editions signal that *Our Nig* was embraced by Wilson's colored brethren, by the late 1850s black patronage for literary pursuits was certainly in place. Nearly two-thirds of black adults in north-

ern cities were at least functionally literate. There were several well-established literary societies in nearby Boston; and though their runs often spanned only several years, a full generation of black newspapers had been launched by this time. Wilson had reason, too, for her specific request for brotherly generosity. While male literary societies supported organizations developed by their sisters, they had also roundly castigated the speaker and essayist Maria Stewart, who broke gendered boundaries by becoming the first American woman to address "promiscuous" audiences and address political themes. By 1833, the outspoken Stewart had been run out of Boston, eventually settling in New York City. See Marilyn Richardson, *Maria W. Stewart, America's First Black Woman Political Writer: Essays and Speeches* (Bloomington: Indiana University Press, 1987); Elizabeth McHenry, *Forgotten Readers: Recovering the Lost History of African American Literary Societies* (Durham, N.C.: Duke University Press, 2002), 68–78; James Oliver Horton and Lois Horton, *In Hope of Liberty: Culture, Community and Protest among Northern Free Blacks, 1700–1860* (New York: Oxford University Press, 1997), 206–7.

CHAPTER I

1. *Mag Smith, My Mother:* This is one of the several first-person references in a text otherwise narrated in the third person and raises the question of whether or not this is a direct autobiographical statement. There is little definitive information about the historical "Mag Smith." Until now, only Harriet's use of the surname "Adams" had given researchers a clue to her mother's married or maiden name. We now know that Wilson's mother's first name was Margaret, which was often at that time shortened to "Mag." And it is also clear that if her parents were married, as outlined in *Our Nig,* then Wilson's maiden name was Green, not Adams. Indeed, her 1870 second marriage records list Wilson's parents as Joshua and Margaret Green; her death certificate lists her father's name, again Joshua Green, but leaves blank "maiden name and birthplace of mother." Suggestively, a March 27, 1830, issue of *Farmer's Cabinet*—the paper that covered the area in which Wilson grew up—reports this death:

> Margaret Ann Smith, black, late of Portsmouth N.H., about 27 years, was found dead in the room of a black man with

> whom she lived in Southack [*sic*] Street, Boston, last week. The verdict of the Coroner's jury was that she came to her death from habitual intoxication. It appears that she and the man had quarreled, both being intoxicated, and he had beaten her severely, but that the immediate cause of her death was drinking half a pint of raw rum.—*The Patriot.*

See introduction for more information.

2. *"Oh, Grief beyond all other griefs . . .":* "Lalla Rookh," in *The Poetical Words of Thomas Moore, Collected by Himself* (Philadelphia: J. P. Lippincott, 1858), 257. Slightly modified from the original verse.
3. *and left her to her fate:* In the condensed opening paragraphs of *Our Nig,* Wilson self-consciously manipulates the tropes of the story of the "fallen woman," the subject of early British and American bestsellers that were still immensely popular during her time. In such stories a teenage girl is often pursued and charmed by a man who is her social and economic superior. In Samuel Richardson's *Pamela* (1740), the servant heroine resists such advances and is rewarded by becoming the bride of "Mr. B.," her employer. In Susannah Rowson's *Charlotte Temple* (1791), the heroine believes her seducer's promises, succumbs, and gives away her "precious" jewel, her virginity, only to be abandoned. These novels went through multiple editions and translations. Black women writers like Wilson and Jacobs incorporate these themes.
4. *Jim:* In pertinent legal documents (Wilson's 1870 marriage certificate and her death certificate), her father's name is listed as Joshua Green. As a "hooper of barrels," Green would have worked either for or with Timothy Blanchard, the head of one of the two households headed by African Americans in Milford. Wilson perhaps borrowed this fictional name from Peter Greene (c. 1750–c. 1836)—possibly her grandfather—who was a blacksmith, farm laborer, and former slave who served in a New York regiment during the Revolutionary War and subsequently settled in Colrain, Massachusetts; he married twice and had several children, including sons Peter Green, Jr. (1787–1865), and James "Jim" Greene (1807–71). Of course, *Our Nig* suggests that "Jim," or Joshua Green, died before 1830. Misspellings of names like Hayward and Green abounded in the nineteenth century; the same families regularly show up in records with modified surnames. See "Pension Application of Peter Green," National Archives.
5. *the Reeds:* Near neighbors of the "Bellmonts," "the Reeds" could represent the families of Calvin Dascomb, Sr., John Blanchard, or

Benjamin Hutchinson, a distant relative of Mrs. Hayward, or "Mrs. Belmont."

6. *Mrs. Bellmont:* Rebecca S. (Hutchinson) Hayward (1780–1850).
7. *Peter Greene:* Timothy Blanchard (1791–1839), a mulatto farmer who owned a cooperage or barrel-making establishment, was born in Wilton, New Hampshire, one of twelve children of George Blanchard (c. 1740–1823), a freed slave and Revolutionary War veteran from Methuen, Massachusetts, who was a noted veterinarian. The family moved to Milford after 1800 and Timothy married Dorcas Hood, a white woman, on August 26, 1820; they would have six sons and two daughters (William Pitt Colburn, "Register," in George Allen Ramsdell, *The History of Milford, New Hampshire, with Family Registers* (Concord, N.H.: Rumford Press, 1901), 485.
8. *Singleton:* The village of Milford, New Hampshire.
9. *"I's black outside, I know, but I's got a white heart inside":* Jim refers to race-based prejudice and to his internal goodness, based on commonplace theological beliefs in God's power to wash away the sins of true Christians and make them clean or "white." "Come now, and let us reason together, saith the Lord: Though your sins be as scarlet, they shall be as white as snow." Isa. 1:18.
10. *the evils of amalgamation:* As the Civil War approached, those who supported the overthrow of slavery and the full enfranchisement of blacks were labeled "amalgamationists" by their political foes. In the early republic, however, whites and blacks of the laboring classes often chose each other as romantic and legal partners. Maryland and Virginia were the first to ratify legal disincentives to interracial couples and to stipulate that the children of enslaved women would occupy the same social standing as their mothers. The interracial children of white women and the white women who chose to partner with black men faced harsh consequences. By 1725–26, Pennsylvania prohibited all interracial unions and remanded any children born to these unions to servitude for thirty-one years. Joel Williamson notes that between 1705 and 1725, all of the colonies from "New Hampshire to South Carolina were coming to legal conclusions not unlike those of Virginia." See Joel Williamson, *New People: Miscegenation and Mulattoes in the United States* (Baton Rouge: Louisiana State University Press, 1995), 8–11; Lorenzo J. Greene, *The Negro in Colonial New England,* 2nd ed. (New York: Antheneum, 1968). See also Martha Hodes, *White Women, Black Men: Illicit Sex in the Nineteenth-Century South* (New Haven: Yale University Press, 1997).

CHAPTER II

1. *My Father's Death:* Another example of first-person usage in a text otherwise told in the third person.
2. *"Misery! we have known each other . . .":* Percy Shelley, "Misery—a Fragment," in *The Poetical Works of Percy Bysshe Shelley, Edited by Mrs. Shelley. With a Memoir,* vol. 2 (New York: Little, Brown, 1835), 399. The epigraph again differs slightly from the original.
3. *victim of consumption:* Consumption was the common name for tuberculosis, a highly contagious lung infection that "consumed" its victims as they wasted away. Consumption was perhaps the most popular literary cause of death for women and children in European and American eighteenth- and nineteenth-century domestic fiction, reflecting the high rates of death for historical victims of the disease. *Uncle Tom's Cabin*'s Little Eva is consumption's most famous literary victim.
4. *the manifestation of Christian patience:* In Christianity, one way in which believers demonstrate their faith is through patience. For example, Rom. 5:2–4 reads: "By whom also we have access by faith into this grace wherein we stand, and rejoice in hope of the glory of God. And not only so, but we glory in tribulations also: knowing that tribulation worketh patience; and patience, experience; and experience, hope."
5. *Seth Shipley:* Not yet identified.
6. *the Bellmonts:* Nehemiah Hayward, Sr. (1738–1825), and his wife, Mary Stickney Hayward (1735–1823), both originally from Rowley, Massachusetts, but more recently from Maugerville, New Brunswick, Canada, landed in the "Duxbury Mile Slip," later Milford, in 1786, with their three surviving children, including Nehemiah, Jr., or "Mr. Bellmont." Hayward, Sr. purchased land, put up a large house, and established a farm. See Matthew A. Stickney, *The Stickney Family: A Genealogical Memoir* (Salem, Mass.: Essex Institute Press, 1869), 451.
7. *John, the son:* Nehemiah Hayward, Jr. (1778–1849), was a well-to-do farmer of Milford, New Hampshire. Interestingly, the name "John Bellmont" closely resembles the name of Sojourner Truth's last owner, John Dumont of Ulster County, New York. This near homonymic link to the master of the most famous former slave woman of the North may be meant to underscore that, despite his

seeming benevolence, Mr. Bellmont is complicit in Frado's involuntary servitude.

8. *A maiden sister shared with him:* The figure of the "maiden" or spinster "aunt" is a standard trope in nineteenth-century women's fiction. The historical Sally Hayward Blanchard, Aunt Abby in *Our Nig,* had been married. When her husband died, she returned to her family. Upon the death of her father in 1825, Sally purchased 59 acres of the family homestead ("an undivided half" of the original property of 118 acres) at "public auction" for seven hundred dollars, thus gaining "the right of occupying one undivided half of all buildings except the barn." Jacob Flynn, administrator of the estate of Nehemiah Hayward, Sr., deceased, to Sally Hayward, Hillsborough County Deed Book 145:493, dated November 10, 1825, recorded November 15, 1825. Her brother had purchased the other 59 acres form his parents some years before. Nehemiah Hayward and Mary his wife to Nehemiah Hayward Jr., Hillsborough County Deed Book 49:47, recorded January 4,1800.

CHAPTER III

1. *A New Home for Me:* Each of the first three chapter titles features first-person usage, while the novel is told in the third person.
2. *"Oh! did we but know of the shadows so nigh . . .":* Eliza Cook, "The Future," in *The Poetical Works of Eliza Cook* (New York: Scribner, Welford, 1870), 187, fourth and fifth stanzas. Wilson's use differs slightly from the published lines.
3. *Mr. B.:* Nehemiah Hayward, Jr., or "Mr. Bellmont." The antagonist in the runaway English bestseller *Pamela* (1740) is also named Mr. B. He is the "master" of the eponymous young servant he attempts to forcibly seduce. *Pamela,* unlike *Our Nig,* however, has a conventional happy ending. Mr. B. falls in love with his servant and marries her.
4. *Mary [Bellmont]:* Rebecca S. Hayward (1822—40), the Haywards' youngest surviving child.
5. *John, or Jack [Bellmont]:* Charles S. Hayward (1818–57), the youngest Hayward son.
6. *"in a few years":* Comments like this suggest that the "Bellmonts" know that it is unusual to put a child to work at the age of six. As Faye Dudden affirms, "orphaned children were commonly bound out at about age ten or twelve to serve until they were eighteen."

Faye E. Dudden, *Serving Women: Household Service in the Nineteenth Century* (Middletown, Conn.: Wesleyan University Press, 1985), 20.

7. *"train up in my way from a child":* Prov. 22:6: "Train up a child in the way he should go: and when he is old, he will not depart from it." This oft-quoted verse from Proverbs underscores the text's ironic commentary on Mrs. B's Christianity. She means to train up Frado in her way, not God's way, to be her servant, rather than God's servant.
8. *Bridget:* Bridget was a common, if disparaging, way to refer generically to Irish women. The first family of Irish immigrants to settle in Milford did so in the 1840s. Ramsdell, *History of Milford,* 189.
9. *how it was* always *to be done:* The text's explicit emphasis on the permanence of Frado's work again underscores the analogy of enslavement rather than indenture as a model for her experience.
10. *"See that nigger":* This description of racial prejudice in Milford, and, by extension, the North, underscores the larger commentary about northern racism that *Our Nig* levels. Mary, not wanting to be seen "walking with a nigger," the text suggests, is hardly exceptional. New Hampshire's most famous ugly episode with black education occurred in 1835 at the interracial, abolitionist-founded Noyes Academy in Canaan, New Hampshire. Wilson's point, of course, is that New Hampshire and its Canaan are no promised land for blacks.
11. *Miss Marsh:* Probably Abby A. (Abigail Atherton) Kent (1802–57), whose mother's family members were prominent residents of the neighboring town of Amherst. The early death of her father, a prominent lawyer and legislator from Chester, New Hampshire, forced Abby to work as a schoolteacher in Amherst and the surrounding areas. She taught school until her 1834 marriage to Robert Means, Jr. By all accounts, Abby Kent Means was a lovely person: warm, tactful, understanding, and sensitive. Her best friend and cousin, Jane Means Appleton, married up-and-coming lawyer Franklin Pierce of Hillsborough, New Hampshire. Pierce was elected U.S. president in 1853; their only surviving child, Benjamin, was killed in a train wreck just before the family left for the D.C. inaugural. Jane Pierce was devastated and unable to fulfill her duties as first lady, so Abby Kent Means stepped in to fill in as White House hostess. When Jane Pierce could again take up the role as first lady, and Mrs. Means had some spare time, she would command the presidential carriage and ride to Myrtilla Miner's "Free Colored Girls' School" (a forerunner of the University of the District of Columbia), where she helped with teaching the girls their

lessons. The local toughs, who verbally and physically harassed the teachers and students as they went about their business, backed off when the carriage with the White House seal on the doors was parked in front of the school, for which Miss Miner, the staff, and students were grateful. See Anne M. Means, *Amherst and Our Family Tree* (Boston: Privately printed, 1921); Myrtilla Miner and Ellen M. O'Connor, *Myrtilla Miner; a Memoir* and *The School for Colored Girls* (1885, 1854, respectively; repr., New York: Arno Press, 1969), 171. Also see Eve Allegra Raimon's "Miss Marsh's Uncommon School Reform" in *Harriet Wilson's New England: Race, Writing, and Region,* eds. Boggis, Raimon, and White. Lebanon, N.H.: University of New Hampshire Press, 2007, 167–82.

12. *referred them to one who looks not on outward appearances, but on the heart:* "The Lord seeth not as man seeth; for man looketh on the outward appearance, but the Lord looketh on the heart." 1 Sam. 16:7.

13. *propping her mouth open:* Beatings on large plantations were often public affairs, and so served both as individual punishment and collective violence done to the enslaved community that was forced to bear witness. In towns, however, slave owners were concerned about both their reputations and accountability; though rarely enforced because blacks were not allowed to serve as witnesses, laws did provide some constraints on violence against slaves. Mrs. B.'s efforts to silence, or privatize, her abuse, by propping Frado's mouth so far open that she could not scream, echoes owners' efforts to keep their abuse quiet. Though Frado is an indentured servant, Mrs. B. does not want to make public the open secret of her abuse by having Frado call attention to Mrs. B.'s violence. Many critics have noted the irony of Frado's mouth being propped open so she won't open her mouth, as it were, concerning Mrs. B.'s behavior.

14. *she was never permitted to shield her skin from the sun:* "Look not upon me, because I am black, because the sun hath looked upon me: my mother's children were angry with me; they made me the keeper of the vineyards; but mine own vineyard have I not kept." Song of Sol. 1:6. Wilson's reference to the Song of Solomon also points to the inequitable distribution of farm work and power that Frado endures at the hands of her "mother's children."

15. *She was not many shades darker than Mary now; what a calamity it would be ever to hear the contrast spoken of:* This reference again links New Hampshire to the slaveholding South and the Bellmont household to southern plantations and homes. Wilson underscores the politics of skin color under which enslaved and le-

gitimate children in the same family resembled each other, while white women would rather not have the family resemblance—or in *Our Nig*'s ironic parlance, the (lack of) "contrast"—spoken of. "The mulattoes one sees in every family partly resemble the white children," lamented South Carolina plantation mistress Mary Boykin Chesnut in her diary. "Any lady is ready to tell you who is the father of all the mulatto children in everybody's household but her own. Those, she seems to think, drop from the clouds." Mary B. Chesnut, *Mary Chesnut's Civil War,* ed. C. Vann Woodward (New Haven: Yale University Press, 1981), 29.

CHAPTER IV

1. *"Hours of my youth! when nurtured in my breast . . .":* George G. N. Byron, 6th Baron Byron, "Childish Recollections," from *Hours of Idleness,* in *The Poetical Works of Lord Byron* (London: John Murray, 1840), 405, second stanza. These lines again differ slightly from the original.
2. *James [Bellmont]:* George Milton Hayward (1807–40), the Haywards' eldest son.
3. *Aunt Abby:* Sarah "Sally" Hayward Blanchard (1776–1859), sister of Nehemiah Hayward, Jr.
4. *Jane [Bellmont]:* Lucretia Hayward (1810–59), the Haywards' second daughter.

CHAPTER V

1. *"Life is a strange avenue of various trees and flowers . . .":* Martin F. Tupper, "Of Life (Second Series)," in *Tupper's Complete Poetical Works* (Boston: Phillips, Sampson, 1850), 192, fourth stanza. Wilson's punctuation and quotation differ from the original.
2. *"cold waters to a thirsty soul":* "As cold waters to a thirsty soul, so is good news from a far country." Prov. 25:25.
3. *Susan:* Nancy Abbot (1810–88) of Wilton, New Hampshire, a schoolteacher and seamstress, married George Milton Hayward on August 16, 1834, in Milford. Abiel Abbot Livermore and Sewell Putnam, *History of the Town of Wilton, Hillsborough County, New Hampshire* (Lowell, Mass.: Marden & Rowell, Printers, 1888), 546.
4. *Henry Reed:* David Hutchinson (1803–81), the eldest surviving son of Jesse Hutchinson, Sr. and Mary "Polly" Leavitt, married

Elizabeth "Betsey," the Haywards' eldest daughter, who had left home before Wilson was abandoned at her parents, and so makes no appearance in *Our Nig*. Though David Hutchinson, or a character based on his relation to Betsey, does not appear in the book, according to contemporaneous statements and the remembrances of his descendants, the portrait of Henry Reed is a highly accurate description of Hutchinson. Like "Henry Reed," he was "tall and spare with red hair and . . . blue eyes" and, again like "Reed," he was known for his parsimony, ability to drive a hard bargain, and propensity to file lawsuits. See John W. Hutchinson, *The Story of the Hutchinsons* (Boston: Lee & Shepard, 1896). Also see Carol R. Brink, *Harps in the Wind* (New York: Macmillan, 1947), 115.

5. *George Means:* Samuel Blanchard (1805–1900) was a native of Rockingham, Vermont; he married Lucretia Hayward (Jane Bellmont) in Milford in 1834; they would have three girls and a boy. Although his father, Jonathan Blanchard, did not have "four wives," as Mrs. B. suggests in her rant against "George Means," Blanchard and his wife, Polly, did have fifteen children, as Mrs. B. loosely complains. One of those children, the Reverend Jonathan Blanchard, Jr. (1811–92), became an abolitionist affiliated with Theodore Dwight Weld and the Lane Seminary radicals. He was a well-known antislavery lecturer traveling throughout the Midwest, who later became the president of Knox College and subsequently founded Wheaton College in Illinois.
6. *procured in a Western City:* Charles Hayward would go "West," as the Midwest was then known, to Bond County, Illinois, with his cousin and brother-in-law Zephaniah Hutchinson in late 1839. On February 29, 1840, Charles purchased forty acres of farmland there. See Bond County Deed Book 146:104, Office of the Bond County Recorder of Deeds, Greenville, Illinois. The 1840 Federal Census lists "C. Haywood [*sic*]," "a white male between the ages of 20–29" (138, line 23).

CHAPTER VI

1. *"Hard are life's early steps . . .":* Wilson transcribed this quote as prose though it originally appears in verse form. Lines by Laetitia Elizabeth Landon, "Success Alone Seen," in *Life and Literary Remains of L.E.L.*, by Laman Blanchard (London: Henry Colburn, 1841), 261.

2. *From early dawn until after all were retired:* This language again strengthens *Our Nig*'s metaphorical and material connections to the conditions of slavery. Enslaved workers labored from "dawn till dusk" or from "sunup till sundown." Of course, their hours were actually much longer as tasks such as food preparation and, for house slaves, domestic labor such as nursing the sick and caring for whites' nighttime needs and desires occupied workers well "after all were retired."
3. *She wore no shoes:* This is a continuous condition for Frado; when she is about seven she goes to school with "scanty clothing and bare feet." In this passage she is about fourteen. This is a familiar trope in African American antislavery materials and slave narratives and so deepens the comparison *Our Nig* forwards. Wilson contradicts more favorable renditions of the North, such as Douglass's affirmation in the 1845 *Narrative* that in the North he saw no "half-naked children and barefooted women." Houston A. Baker, Jr., *Narrative of the Life of Frederick Douglass, An American Slave* (New York: Penguin Classics, 1982), 148.
4. *shaved her glossy ringlets . . . anything but an enticing object:* There are several literary instances of mistresses shaving mulattas' hair. In *Clotel* (1853), the narrator describes how "every married woman in the far South looks upon her husband as unfaithful, and regards every quadroon servant as a rival. Clotel had been with her now but a few days, when she was ordered to cut off her long hair." See William Wells Brown, *Clotel, or, The President's Daughter,* edited with introduction and notes by M. Giulia Fabi (1853, London: Partridge & Oakey; repr., New York: Penguin, 2004), 121.

CHAPTER VII

1. *"What are our joys but dreams . . .":* "Time, A Poem," in *The Complete Poetical Works of Henry Kirke White* (Boston: N. H. Whitaker, 1931), 136, third stanza, lines 3–4.

CHAPTER VIII

1. *"Other cares engross me . . .":* "Written in the Prospect in Death," in *The Poetical Works of Henry Kirke White* (London: Bell and Daldy, 1830), 9. Wilson takes certain liberties with her citation.

2. *Lewis [Bellmont]:* Jonas Hutchinson Hayward (1814–66) left Milford for Baltimore in 1836; he took his brother's failing stove business and turned it into an American industrial giant. With his brother Nehemiah, he patented a number of innovations for cooking stoves and perfected home heating systems, circulatory systems, fire hydrants, and plumbing fixtures. The firm, which became Bartlett Hayward & Company, employed thousands during its heyday, and still exists as a subsidiary of Koppers Corporation.
3. *Susan and Charlie:* Caroline Frances Hayward (1836–89) was the only child of George and Nancy Hayward; she never married. This is one of the few direct discrepancies in the text, although "Charlie" is an obvious quasi-homonymic nickname for Caroline.
4. *veil of doubt and sin:* In the New Testament, the veil metaphorically describes the inability to understand the spiritual truth one needs in order to accept Christ. See 2 Cor. 3:16.
5. *to the communion of the saints:* Christians often refer to followers of Christ, or the body of believers, as "the saints." See, for example, 1 Thess. 3:13.
6. *"we should very soon have her in the parlor":* In sentimental fiction, the middle-class parlor had particular significance as the heart of the home; indeed it symbolized safety and domestic civilization, a place protected from the "pollution" of the public sphere. Mrs. B. strives to keep everyone she sees as illegitimate out of the parlor. She is later irritated by Aunt Abby's "impudence in presenting herself unasked in the parlor."
7. *prayer of the publican, "God be merciful to me a sinner":* In Luke 18:13, when the publican prays, as Frado here does, "God, be merciful to me a sinner," he humbles himself, in direct contrast to the Pharisee who in prayer displays only self-righteousness and self-satisfaction. In this parable Jesus teaches: "every one that exalteth himself shall be abased" (Luke 18:14). As those who know the Bible would realize, the line Wilson quotes is followed directly by one of the Bible's best-known phrases: "suffer little children to come unto me, and forbid them not: for of such is the kingdom of God" (Luke 18:16). Readers who share Wilson's religious training would catch the extended irony of her biblical citation.

CHAPTER IX

1. *"We have now but a small portion of what men call time, to hold communion":* "Written in the Prospect of Death," in *The Poetical*

Works of Henry Kirke White (London: Bell and Daldy, 1830), 79. Wilson's citation of the lines again differs from the original.

2. *"If she minded her mistress, and did what she commanded, it was all that was required of her":* Coloss. 3:22: "Servants, obey in all things your masters." Paul's biblical admonition to servants was a popular verse with slavery's supporters. Abolitionists often reference its recital by masters and their preachers to highlight Christian hypocrisy. Though in the third person, Wilson quotes Mrs. B. and so further links her to the "professed Christians" mocked in the abolitionist press and in slave narratives.
3. *the Angel of Death severed the golden thread:* This passage paraphrases Eccles. 12:6–7, which reads "or ever the silver cord be loosed, or the golden bowl be broken . . . then shall the dust return to the earth as it was: and the spirit shall return unto God who gave it."

CHAPTER X

1. *"Neath the billows of the ocean . . .":* According to Ellis, this epigraph may be from George W. Cook's *The Mariner's Physician and Surgeon; or a Guide to the Homeopathic Treatment of Those Diseases to Which Seamen are Liable, Comprising the Treatment of Syphilitic Diseases etc.* (New York: J.T.S. Smith, 1848). Reginald Pitts suggests that it is as likely the work of George Washington Light (1809–68) who was a Boston book publisher of progressive titles, the editor of several papers including the *Colonizationist* and the *Journal of Freedom,* and an author of poetry and biography. He was active in antislavery and early trade union movements. His book, *Keep Cool, Go Ahead and a Few Other Poems* (1851), does not include this verse, which may have been published in New England newspapers or elsewhere.
2. *"bruised reed":* In quoting Matt. 12:20, "a bruised reed shall he not break," the text foregrounds Mr. B.'s recuperation from his loss. Mr. B. now fosters Frado's religious education.
3. *narrow way:* The "narrow way" commonly refers to the path of Christ that leads to salvation. See Matt. 7:14: "Because strait is the gate, and narrow is the way, which leadeth unto life, and few there be that find it."
4. *"She got into the* river *again . . . the Jordan is a big one to tumble into":* Jordan is both the river in which John the Baptist baptizes

Christ and the symbolic boundary between slavery and freedom reflected in black spirituals. The text suggests that even the river Jordan cannot wash away Mary's sins; her black heart will make her a "nigger."

5. *so detestable a plague:* Note the similarity in Harriet Jacobs's indictment of her master and Wilson's of her "mistress." Jacobs writes: "O, how I despised him! I thought how glad I should be, if some day when he walked the earth, it would open and swallow him up, and disencumber the world of a plague." *Incidents in the Life of a Slave Girl,* ed. Jean Fagan Yellin (Cambridge: Harvard University Press, 1987), 18.
6. *she was restrained by an overruling Providence:* Hagar, Sarai/Sarah's black Egyptian handmaid, flees from her mistress's harsh treatment. An angel meets her and tells her that the Lord hears her affliction, and that her seed shall be multiplied, but that she should nonetheless go back to Sarah, saying, "Return to thy mistress, and submit thyself under her hands." Gen. 16:8–10.

CHAPTER XI

1. *"Crucified the hopes that cheered me . . ." C. E.:* The Anglo-Irish writer whose *nom de plume* was Charlotte Elizabeth (1790–1846) may be the author of the epigraph attributed to "C. E." Her tracts, novels, and poetry were very popular in the United States and Britain. Among them were the antislavery novel *The System* (1827) and a number of working-class novels including *Helen Fleetwood* (1840). *The Wrongs of Women* (1844) is considered to be her major work. She was the editor of the *Christian Lady's Magazine* (1833–36) and of the *Protestant Magazine* (1841–46). Harriet Beecher Stowe edited *The Collected Works of Charlotte Elizabeth* in 1849. Charlotte Elizabeth Brown married a Captain Phelan, an abusive drunk whom she left. When he died, she remarried Lewis H. J. Tonna, who was twenty-one years her junior.
2. *Jenny:* Sarah Ann Newby, originally from Virginia (1822–51), married Charles S. Hayward (Jack) on April 1, 1841, in Bond County, Illinois. Their son, George Milton Hayward II (1844–81), was taken in by his Uncle Jonas in Baltimore and trained in the family business of selling stoves. See 1880 Federal Census for Washington, D.C., sheet 237-A. Also see Bond County, Illinois, marriage book 1:34, Bond County Historical Society, Greenville, Illinois.

3. *Mrs. Smith:* One of the near neighbors of the Haywards/Bellmonts—possibly Mrs. Rachel Putnam Dascomb, wife of Calvin Dascomb, Sr.
4. *Mrs. Moore:* Not identified. Possibly named for Mrs. Mary J. French Moore (1808–98), second wife of the Reverend Humphrey Moore, the abolitionist pastor of the Congregationalist Church in Milford (1802–36) who married the Haywards and later became an antislavery state representative.
5. *Mrs. Hale:* Perhaps Sarah Dexter Kimball (b. 1816) who was the wife of Reverend Lycurgus Kimball (1814–51), who pastored the Milford Congregational Church from 1847 to 1849. They had two children, Edwin and Harriette Louise. The latter child's birth, on September 26, 1846, may be referenced in *Our Nig,* when Wilson uses "additional cares" to describe the extra burden of childcare. See Ramsdell, *History of Milford,* 198; Leonard A. Morrison and Stephen P. Sharples, *History of the Kimball Family from 1634 to 1897* (Boston: Amrell & Upham, 1897), 520; 1850 Federal Census for Rushville Corporation, Schuyler County, Illinois, sheet 8, lines 31–34.
6. *Mrs. Hoggs:* Possibly Mary Louise (Barnes) Boyles (1811–92), originally of Goffstown; she married Samuel Boyles (1806–71) in 1830 and they had three children. Mrs. Boyles took in both boarders and paupers, as stated in the 1850 Federal Census return for Milford that features "Harriet Adams" (later Harriet E. Wilson) and also the 1860 and 1870 Federal Census returns for Milford where there are a number of unrelated persons in the Boyles household. Suggestively, the Boyleses may have been Spiritualists; Samuel Boyles's tombstone in the West Street Cemetery in Milford states that he was "translated to the Spirit World." A number of Milford tombstones marking the last resting place of known Spiritualists bear similar inscriptions. Visit by Gabrielle Foreman and Reginald Pitts to West Street Cemetery, October 2003.

CHAPTER XII

1. *"Nothing new under the sun":* "The thing that hath been, it is that which shall be; and that which is done is that which shall be done: and there is no new thing under the sun." Eccles. 1:9.
2. *within the compass of my narrative:* The only first-person usage within the body of the narrative itself.
3. *professed fugitives:* Harriet Wilson was not an exception in exposing the attraction of posing as a "fugitive" when faced with the

stunning lack of economic opportunities free blacks confronted in the United States. Nor was "Samuel" or Thomas Wilson alone; several "professed fugitives," as Wilson puts it in the plural, traveled throughout New England and the Middle Atlantic States, giving "lectures" and soliciting. In 1854, *London's Anti-Slavery Reporter* ran a column titled "Colored Lecturers—Caution" that warned: "We have to caution the public—and especially our anti-slavery friends—against certain coloured men who are now going through the country . . . delivering lectures on American Slavery, temperance, and other subjects." They "strongly recommend our friends, throughout the country, not to give countenance to any individuals professing to be fugitive slaves, unless the latter present some satisfactory recommendations, and can give an account of themselves and of the manner in which they reached the country, which will bear investigation. Whilst we would not, on any account, divert benevolence from a worthy object, we feel it incumbent upon us to do all that lies in our power to prevent it from being practised upon." The *Liberator* also printed a number of articles warning the public against pretended fugitive slaves. See *London's Anti-Slavery Reporter,* March 1, 1854.

4. *Samuel was kind to her when at home, but made no provision for his absence:* Some variation of women being left to their own support was not uncommon when men left their families to lecture, as on the antislavery circuit, or to work. Douglass, William Craft, and Martin Delany, for example, took extended trips away from home, leaving their wives to manage household affairs and finances. In *Black Jacks: African American Seaman in the Age of Sail* (Cambridge: Harvard University Press, 1997), 171, W. Jeffrey Bolster notes a number of instances where the wives and children of men long at sea were forced to apply for help from the Overseers of the Poor in the towns and cities where they lived.
5. *illiterate harangues were humbugs for hungry abolitionists:* Critics agree that these references, which paint abolitionists as overeager dupes, may in part explain why *Our Nig* was never reviewed in the abolitionist press. The movement had been hurt by the fake narrative that James Williams had dictated to an unwitting John Greenleaf Whittier, which appeared in the February 1838 *Anti-Slavery Examiner.* As Henry Louis Gates, Jr. puts it, the narrative was "so compelling, so gripping, so *useful* . . . that the abolitionists decided to publish it and distribute it widely, sending copies to every state and to every congressman" before it was exposed and they were forced to issue retractions. Likewise, the *London Anti-Slavery Reporter* warned that such imposters "lay their plans with

an especial view to this practise upon those whom they are aware are already pre-disposed to listen to a skillfully-invented and well-told tale of woe, and suffering, and hair-breadth escapes." Wilson echoes the paper's observation that "if anti-slavery friends would, as a rule, observe a little more caution, imposters would not find it so easy to make dupes." As Suzanne Schneider points out, the very popular P. T. Barnum was known as the "prince of humbug" at this time; Wilson's language calls attention to the issues of commodification, spectatorship, and sensationalism that haunted the display of black Americans as speakers on the antislavery circuit. See Henry Louis Gates, Jr., "From Wheatley to Douglass: The Politics of Displacement," in *Frederick Douglass: New Literary and Historical Essays,* ed. Eric J. Sundquist (New York: Cambridge University Press, 1990), 59; and *London's Anti-Slavery Reporter,* March 1, 1854. Schneider, private conversation with Gabrielle Foreman, April 2004.

6. *Then followed the birth of her child:* George Mason Wilson was born at the Hillsborough County Poor Farm in Goffstown in late May or early June 1852, possibly June 15 of that year. Although it is likely that he could have been named for George Mason Hayward ("James Bellmont"), it is of interest that the baby bears the same name as (Caleb) George Mason Hutchinson (1844–93), the only son of Caleb and Laura Wright Hutchinson. Caleb was an elder brother of the Singing Hutchinson Family, and his own son was called "George" most of his life in order to distinguish him from his father. It is possible that Caleb and Laura, or his twin, Joshua, with his wife, Irene Fisher Hutchinson, may have cared for young George Wilson. The 1860 Census shows that Joshua Hutchinson took in paupers, for which he was presumably compensated by the town. See 1860 Federal Census for Town of Milford. See also 1850 Federal Census for Milford, Hillsborough County, 377: 1860 Federal Census for Milford, 126; Colburn, "Register," in *History of Milford,* 788.
7. *As soon as her babe could be nourished . . . she left him in charge:* Nineteenth-century readers would have understood Wilson's decision to leave her son in someone else's charge so that she would be able to gain a livelihood that could support them both. "Women whose marriages had failed had to give up their children in order to enter domestic service, leaving them with relatives, boarding them, or binding them out." Dudden, *Serving Women,* 206.
8. *Mrs. Capon:* Not yet identified.
9. *Watched by kidnappers:* Free-born and self-emancipated blacks in the North faced a precarious situation after the compromise of

1850 and its Fugitive Slave provision was passed. Financial incentives at every stage encouraged remanding back to slavery people who were identified as runaways, whatever their actual legal status. Instead of jury trials, special commissioners heard cases; they were paid five dollars if an alleged fugitive were released and ten dollars if he or she were returned south.

10. *maltreated by professed abolitionists:* Wilson's assertion is in line with white antislavery and women's rights advocate Sarah Grimké's report on racial discrimination among Quakers. In 1839, Grimké describes a woman's confession that in her household the black hired hand was given separate dishes. The family "'would no more have thought of using them, than if a cat or dog had eaten with them'—Such said she 'are the prejudices I was educated in, I have found it hard to overcome them.'" Wilson's commentary underscores that even the most egalitarian communities would often mistreat blacks in their midst. Carolyn Williams, "The Female Antislavery Movement: Fighting against Racial Prejudice and Promoting Women's Rights in Antebellum America," in *The Abolitionist Sisterhood: Women's Political Culture,* ed. Jean Fagan Yellin and John C. Van Horne (Ithaca: Cornell University Press), 167.

11. *Traps slyly laid by the vicious to ensnare her:* Traps by the vicious could refer to plots to enslave free blacks, plots to sexually ensnare impoverished women, or a combination of the two.

12. *gentle reader:* This form of direct address is commonly employed in domestic fiction.

13. *as Joseph from the butler's, but she will never cease to track them till beyond mortal vision:* In *Our Nig*'s closing passage, Frado is positioned as the biblical Joseph, a spiritually powerful and unjustly enslaved reader of dreams who will eventually escape and prosper (Gen. 40:23). This last reference to Joseph portends Wilson's future as a well-respected and serious practitioner of Spiritualism, where in trances, mediums communicated with those in the "spirit world."

APPENDIX

1. *itinerant colored lecturer:* Possibly Thomas H. Jones (1806–c. 1865), an escaped slave from Wilmington, North Carolina, who published his story, *The Experience of Thomas H. Jones, Who was a Slave for Forty-Three Years,* in three printings (1854, 1862, 1865). He was also a Baptist minister and lecturer based in Salem

and Worcester, Massachusetts. Jones gave public talks about his life as a slave until May 1851 when, upon the enactment of the Fugitive Slave Act, he fled to Canada and Great Britain, where he stayed for almost two years. He later returned to Worcester, where he stayed until 1862, before relocating to Boston's Sixth Ward.

2. *Mrs. Walker:* Possibly Mary Wrigley Walker (1798–1871), a native of Rochdale, Lancashire, England, who emigrated to America with her husband Matthew about 1820, settling first in Charlstown, Massachusetts, then in Stow, Massachusetts, and then Providence, Rhode Island, before moving to Ware, Massachusetts, the "W—— Mass." where Wilson almost surely spent time as a "straw sewer" in the 1850s. Walker's last years were spent in Harwick, Massachusetts.
3. *"black, but comely":* "I am black, but comely, O ye daughters of Jerusalem, as the tents of Kedar, as the curtains of Solomon. Look not upon me, because I am black; because the sun hath looked upon me. My mother's children were angry with me, they made me the keeper of the vineyards, but mine own vineyard have I not kept." Song of Sol. 1:5–6.
4. *"My cup runneth over":* "Thou preparest a table before me in the presence of mine enemies: thou anointest my head with oil; my cup runneth over. Surely goodness and mercy shall follow me all the days of my life: and I will dwell in the house of the Lord for ever." Ps. 23:5–6.
5. *"it is not in man that walketh to direct his steps":* Jer. 10:23.
6. *"rich in faith":* "Hearken, my beloved brethren, Hath not God chosen the poor of this world rich in faith, and heirs of the kingdom which he hath promised to them that love him? But ye have despised the poor. Do not rich men oppress you, and draw you before the judgment seats? Do not they blaspheme that worthy name by the which ye are called?" James 2:5–7.
7. *County House:* The Hillsborough County Poor Farm was established in Goffstown, New Hampshire, in 1849, in order to "house the county poor," who at that time numbered about ninety. The buildings burned in 1866, and the farm was moved to the Whiting Farm in Wilton in April 1867, and still later to the hamlet of Grasmere, just outside of Goffstown. See George Plummer Hadley, *History of the Town of Goffstown, New Hampshire, 1733–1920* (Concord, N.H.: Published for the Town of Goffstown, 1924), 424–27; Livermore and Putnam, *History of the Town of Wilton,* 176–80.
8. *"'prophet's chamber,' except there was no 'candlestick'":* "Let us make a little chamber, I pray thee, on the wall; and let us set for him

there a bed, and a table, and a stool, and a candlestick: and it shall be, when he cometh to us, that he shall turn in thither." 2 Kings 5:10. "Allida" is quoting here from a letter from Wilson. It is a reference to the story of a Shunamite woman, from a tribe that is recognized as "black and comely," who invites a poor stranger, the prophet Elisha, to stay in her home. She and her husband build him a modest "chamber" where he can stay during his journeys; and the prophet, in turn, promises the woman a son, yet he dies as a young boy. The couple appeals to Elisha, who returns to pray over the boy who has been laid out in Elisha's chamber. Elisha revives the child, at which time the relieved mother "went in, and fell at his feet, and bowed herself to the ground, and took up her son, and went out." 2 Kings 5:37. Wilson's reference in this letter typifies her narrative strategies. She occupies the place of both Elisha, for whom the modest prophet chamber is constructed, and the Shunamite, the black female protagonist of the story. These verses, and the ways in which she complicates them, eerily anticipate her own experience, though Wilson's lacked a happy ending. Wilson and her soon-to-be-born son end up back in the prophet's chamber, in this case, the County House; he dies as a child, and though she tries to save him, to take up her son and go out, young George is never revived.

9. *"'I am poor and needy'":* "But I am poor and needy; yet the Lord thinketh upon me: thou art my help and my deliverer; make no tarrying, O my God." Ps. 40:17.

10. *A kind gentleman and lady:* Possibly Joshua Hutchinson (1811–83) and his wife, Irene Fisher Hutchinson (1810–88). Joshua was the leader of the Hutchinson "Home Branch," those members of the Family Singers who performed throughout New England while the more famous siblings traveled throughout the United States and Europe. Joshua was actively antislavery and the family regularly hosted black guests and abolitionist speakers. As the family took care of town paupers, they would have been perfect candidates to care for George Wilson and treat him well, as "Allida" suggests.

11. *"at the resurrection of the just":* "But when thou makest a feast, call the poor, the maimed, the lame, the blind. And thou shalt be blessed; for they cannot recompense thee: for thou shalt be recompensed at the resurrection of the just." Luke 14:13–14.

12. *bestowed a recipe upon her for restoring gray hair to its former color:* There were a number of "recipes" used by antebellum hairdressers and barbers; this "recipe" could have been provided by an African American barber in a town she may have visited—William H. Montague of Springfield, Massachusetts, or Phillip O.

Ames of Nashua, for example. See chronology notes for more information.

13. *Autobiography:* Though *Our Nig*'s maneuvers are clearly novelistic, the facts it relates are as clearly autobiographical. Within the text, *Our Nig* is referred to as "sketches" or as an "autobiography."
14. *"I will help thee, saith the Lord":* "I will help thee, saith the Lord, and thy redeemer, the Holy One of Israel." Isa. 41:14.
15. *Allida or "Aunt J":* Possibly Jane Chapman (Maslen) Demond (1814–1904); originally from North Bradley, Wiltshire, England, Jane emigrated with her family to New York City when she was in her teens. On June 30, 1841, she married Lorenzo Demond (1812–73) of Spencer, Massachusetts; they would have three children. In 1845, they moved to Ware, Massachusetts, where Lorenzo operated a large farm as well as a "bonnet-making manufactory." He hired local women to stitch together straw hats at their homes; this is the work Harriet does in W——, Massachusetts, until her health again fails. The 1850 Federal Census Enumeration of Population for the village of Ware does not show any women with the occupation of "straw sewer"; the 1860 Census shows twenty women who listed their occupation as "sews straw."
16. *She was indeed a slave, in every sense of the word:* An 1857 New Hampshire law declared that any person "who held or attempted to hold a person in slavery, should be deemed guilty of felony, and on conviction to be confined to hard labor not less than one, nor more than five years." J. W. Hammonds, "Slavery in New Hampshire," *Magazine of American History with Notes and Queries* 21 (January–June 1889), 65. Though Rebecca Hutchinson Hayward ("Mrs. B.") had died in 1850, Wilson's excoriation and the confirmation of "Margaretta Thorn," published just two years after New Hampshire's passage of such a law, carries the force not only of their conviction, but threatens to merge moral and legal indictments.
17. *and a lonely one, too:* Most young women working in single-servant households "found the isolation of domestic service extremely painful." Three-quarters of the domestics in Providence in 1855, for example, worked under such arrangements, as had 45 percent in Boston in 1845. Most domestics in urban settings socialized with others in the nearby vicinity, despite their employers' complaints and attempts to undermine their efforts. While Wilson was not the only servant employed on the Hayward farm, she was the only indentured and house servant in a rural setting and her loneliness would have been further magnified by her racial isolation. See Dudden, *Serving Women,* 197–98.

18. *inasmuch as ye have done a good deed:* "Verily I say unto you, Inasmuch as ye have done it unto one of the least of these my brethren, ye have done it unto me." Matt. 25:40.
19. *while the day lasts, and we shall in no wise lose our reward:* "And if anyone gives even a cup of cold water to one of these little ones because he is my disciple, I tell you the truth, he will certainly not lose his reward." Matt. 10:42. This references what is commonly called the "last days," when God will account for His children's good deeds.
20. *Margaretta Thorn:* Possibly Laura Wright Hutchinson of Milford, wife of Caleb Hutchinson, part of the Milford Hutchinson clan and later a noted Spiritualist medium. The writer is almost certainly a resident of Milford or the immediate area, personally knew Wilson's story very well, and obviously sympathized with her.
21. *C. D. S.:* Though Henry Louis Gates, Jr. and Barbara A. White suggest that "C. D. S." stands for the legal abbreviation "Colored Indentured Servant," the term was used primarily, and perhaps only, in Ohio. More probably this is Calvin Dascomb, Sr. (1790–1859), who farmed in the towns of Milford and Wilton, and was married to Rachel Putnam of Wilton (1796–1856), a first cousin once removed of Nancy A. Hayward ("Susan Bellmont"). Dascomb was a near neighbor of the Haywards for many years and thus would have known Harriet from the time she arrived at the Haywards' through her marriage and her son's birth. See Livermore and Putnam, *History of the Town of Wilton,* 360, 479, 527; Colburn, "Register," in *History of Milford,* 666.